JUST A NOTE FROM THE AUTHOR

Back in the mid-eighties, I wrote *Texas Anthem*. It was the first of a family saga set against the western frontier from the end of the Mexican-American War to the turn of the century. *Texas Born* ~~saw a fi~~ ～～～～ us forward several years ~~～～～～～～～～～～～～～～～～～～～～～~~ *as Anthem*. We've watch ~~～～～～～～～～～～～～～~~ successful and respected ~~～～～～～～～～～~~ out of the wilds of West ~~～～～～～～～～~~ daughter, all of them m ~~～～～～～～～～~~ ～～ for their parents as we've discovered. I am pleased that St. Martin's Press is reprinting all five novels in the series.

The Anthem family is a robust collection of men and women shaped by the land, a strong and independent breed, often flawed and perhaps too headstrong, but the kind of folks who will stand for justice, live life to the fullest, and cast a tall shadow.

Shadow Walker is set just after the Civil War. John Anthem's proud but wayward young son, Cole Tyler Anthem, has yet to return home. That terrible conflict which saw the destruction of the Confederacy has made its mark upon young Cole, leaving wounds both of the spirit and the flesh. But Cole Anthem will have to heal himself if he is to survive his encounter with a ghostly killer who stalks the hills of Arkansas, a savage specter who strikes swiftly and vanishes without a trace. Is it a man or some supernatural beast, this thing called *Shadow Walker*?

* * *

I reckon this is where I'm expected to tell you how I lived a life of towering adventure, saddle-broke a hundred wild mustangs, pitched a tent in Tibet, hunted Cape buffalo, served with distinction, rode with the wind, trampled the wild places and the crooked highways . . . oh, heck with it. That's not me.

I was the kid who sat in the front row of the balcony of the movie theater and spent every Saturday afternoon with the likes of John Wayne, Burt Lancaster, Kirk Douglas, Lee Marvin, Charlton Heston, Gregory Peck, and the list goes on; a kid who thrilled to the sight of charging Comanches, saloon brawls, and shoot-outs in dusty streets, not to mention sword fights, heroic last stands, dueling pirate ships, and chariot races. And when I wasn't at the theater, I was reading the same, yondering by way of the written word, finding the lost and lonely places, and dreaming I would one day be the tale-teller, spinning legends on the wheel of my imagination.

Sure, I've done some things, been some places. But so have you. All that matters now, my friend, is the story we share. I have tried to craft these books with a sense of legend as well as history; finding just the right blend of thrills, drama, romance, and a dash of wit. Whether or not I have succeeded is in your hands.

WELCOME TO TEARDROP

COLE FELT A TINGE OF REGRET. He liked O'Brian's spirit. The Kid had lived a wildfire life. Now civilized society demanded that he pay. And Cole Anthem was the instrument of society, of justice. Yet, what justice robbed a people of their homeland and birthright?

Cole willed away such speculation. He was bringing a man in for a reward. It was as simple as that. He crossed the room. Time to see to the horses and find a meal. As Cole flung open the front door, he found himself staring down the muzzle of a shotgun. Half a dozen other rifles and Colt revolvers were cocked simultaneously. The man with the shotgun was as tall as Cole, a few years older with thinning hair, and a jaw that looked solid as granite. He sighted down the shotgun.

A short, wiry young man stepped out of the crowd, raised his Colt, thumbed the hammer back, pressed the gun to Anthem's heart and said:

"Welcome to Teardrop, you son of a bitch."

SHADOW WALKER

KERRY NEWCOMB

St. Martin's Paperbacks

PUBLISHER'S NOTE

This book is a work of fiction. Names, characters, places, and incidents either are the product of the author's imagination or are used fictitiously, and any resemblance to actual persons, living or dead, events, or locales is entirely coincidental.

SHADOW WALKER

Copyright © 1987 by James Reno.
"Just a Note From the Author" copyright © 2001 by Kerry Newcomb.

ISBN: 0-312-97884-7

Printed in the United States of America

Signet edition / August 1987
St. Martin's Paperbacks edition / June 2001

St. Martin's Paperbacks are published by St. Martin's Press, 175 Fifth Avenue, New York, NY 10010.

10 9 8 7 6 5 4 3 2 1

*This novel is for Patty and Amy Rose
and Paul Joseph with love*

I would like to thank Tex Crowell for giving me a crash course in the formation and location of diamonds.

And Aaron Priest, how can I ever thank you enough for being the terrific agent that you are.

My gratitude too for the patience and expertise of Maureen Baron and the good people at NAL.

And a heartfelt *adiós* to Max and Bob and Crash wherever you are.

SHADOW WALKER

★

PROLOGUE

NOVEMBER 1866

The body seemed to take forever to fall. The legs splayed out, arms fluttered as it performed an ungainly somersault. There was a crackle and snap of barren branches, then a muffled thud as the body struck ground.

It was a hell of a way for Matt Behan to end a hunt.

Matt's sons were climbing the slope below when they saw their father fall. Fearing the worst, they worked their way up through big timber until they found the body. Matt Behan, a man of power and prominence in life, was dead, brought down just a month shy of fifty years old.

Jordan Behan, Matt's eldest son, stood off to the side, speechless at the sight of his father's broken frame. Ezra Behan, younger by a couple of years, knelt by his father's side to inspect the corpse.

"That's damn peculiar," Ezra muttered.

"Pa's dead, Ezra. Must you number his bones? They look all broken. And there's his rifle, bent to hell." Jordan pointed to the gun where it lay, bent and broken on an ice-flecked ledge. He glanced at the corpse again. "Cover him and let's bring him home to Mother." Jordan frowned. "Peculiar? How do you mean?" He drew closer, his big frame casting a shadow over his father's corpse.

To Jordan's horror, Ezra pried open the dead man's jaws, reached in, and pulled out a rounded crystalline stone about the size of a thumbnail. He wiped it clean of blood. The stone had lodged in the dead man's cheek on impact.

"What kind of fall slits a man's throat from ear to ear?" Ezra said. "And stuffs this in his mouth?" Ezra held out the stone for his older brother's examination.

Jordan swore.

It was a diamond.

1

APRIL 1867

Blue Elk O'Brian laughed at the men who were trying
to kill him. He clung to his concealed perch in the
lofty branches of an oak tree and watched as the Regulators lined themselves on the crest of a limestone
ridge, then continued down toward him, following the
circuitous trail he had left for them. O'Brian, better
known as the Osage Kid, brushed his shaggy black
hair out of his eyes and grinned. He adjusted his
weight, being careful not to disturb the swarm of bees
at the end of the branch he had sawed almost completely through. Supporting the weight of the branch
and massive hive with his left arm, O'Brian braced
himself by shoving his right foot against a nearby
branch and worked himself deeper into the cleft of the
trunk. As yet, the mass of bees hadn't noticed him.
O'Brian's build was small, unlike that of most Osage
men, and he was able to blend into the shadowy re-

cesses of the tree. He had wrapped himself in a faded
brown blanket to better conceal his beaded buckskin
shirt and Confederate-issue britches.

His fingers absently played with the mussel-shell
necklace circling his throat as he watched the three
troopers riding toward him.

The officer in the lead, Major Andrew Kedd, wore
a blue felt hat that trailed a black plume. The thin,
delicately built Regulator rode as if he were on parade. As he paused to study the tracks leading down
the hillside into the grove of oak trees, Kedd removed
his hat and brushed back a shock of prematurely silver
hair. A silver goatee added emphasis to an already
jutting jaw. Kedd replaced his hat and motioned for
the two men behind him to follow as he continued
down the slope. The other two Regulators looked wor-
riedly from one to the other. The Ozarks were hardly
things of beauty to them. These forested ridges and
dark hollows were places to be avoided.

A man could wind up real dead hereabouts. And
the only thing worse than being dead was being *real*
dead. Everybody knew that.

Their voices carried to the Osage Kid in the treetop.

"Major Kedd, sir, meaning no disrespect, but
shouldn't we be waiting for the rest of the men to find
us," the bolder of the two, Corporal J. D. Canton,
called out.

The man at his side, middle-aged like the corporal
but without any ranking, rubbed his reddened cheeks.
He needed a drink. Hell, Pepper Fisk always needed
a drink. "J. D.'s got a point, Major, sir."

Kedd did not bother to reply but waved the men onward. "Come along, lads. We'll skin this half-breed buck today. Mark my word we'll shoot him down like the disreputable savage he is or truss him up and ship him off to Indian territory the same as we did the rest of the red devils."

"Yes sir." Fisk found the courage to continue the argument. "But he's gone and scattered the boys over half of almighty creation . . . and left just us three . . ." He searched the forest ahead, his gaze wide eyed and worried.

"That's quite enough, Private Fisk."

Pepper Fisk swallowed a retort and glanced aside at the corporal, who shook his head.

"Show some backbone, Pepper," the corporal growled as if he had never complained. He flexed his big beefy shoulders and flashed a yellow-toothed wicked smile that added no warmth to his grizzled features.

Sideburns thick as briar patches covered his cheeks. Beneath his hat, his bald skull was dotted with sweat. Moisture glistened in the graying sideburns. A ragged scar cut a crescent moon just beneath his right eye.

Pepper rubbed a hand over his thick fleshy lips and veined cheeks. His bulbous nose twitched as he sniffed the air in hopes of discovering the scent of a campfire. His rounded belly growled, but his thoughts weren't of food. Only of the taste of the rye whiskey the corporal had concealed in his saddlebags.

The three men reached a dry watercourse and, keeping to the winding ribbon of hoofprints, continued on into the shade. There the spring air brushed cool against their features and the land waited in mystery, for the tracks in the soft earth indicated their quarry had experienced some confusion as to the path ahead. No tracks led away. They simply stopped.

"What the devil is this?" said Andrew Kedd.

J. D. Canton and Pepper Fisk were busy trying to make some sense out of the tracks beneath the tree. They never had a chance to reply. Up above, the Osage Kid slashed down with his broad blade—fourteen inches of double-edged steel honed to a razor-sharpness—and severed the branch at its base. The branch dropped like a rock carrying its burden of newly swarmed bees right into the middle of the Regulators. The cluster of insects exploded and attacked both horse and rider in their agitated state. As the bees found their target, O'Brian ducked beneath his blanket to keep from being stung. Kedd, Fisk, and Canton yelled and batted at the insects. Their horses neighed and reared and kicked the air teeming with furious bugs. All three horses bolted as one away from the woods and headed at a gallop toward the slope. They took the incline without breaking stride as the bees swarmed after them. Fisk howled the loudest as stinger after stinger lanced his skin. Corporal Canton bellowed like a bear. Kedd bore his pain and suffering in silence until the last minute, when a peculiarly vengeful bee found his ear and thrust deep. The major straightened in the saddle, slapped at his head, and rent the afternoon with a piercing cry that turned to a curse levied against O'Brian.

When the troopers had vanished in the distance beyond the hills, the Osage Kid took his chances and scampered down the oak. He darted away from the tree and followed the deer trail deep into the woods.

He found his horse where he had left the animal, ground-tethered near a bubbling spring. O'Brian knelt by the chestnut and unwrapped the strips of cloth he had tied on its legs to soften the imprint of the shod hooves in the soft earth. The animal continued to crop the tender shoots of sweet spring grass growing around the edge of the spring.

When O'Brian finished unwrapping the hooves, he pulled up the stake he had driven into the ground, and patted the gelding's neck. "Looks like we won again," he said softly. Taking reins in hand, he swung up into the Confederate-issue saddle.

O'Brian had skirmished with Major Kedd on several occasions, ever since the Yankee major had arrived in Arkansas with his force of military police, men from both sides of the Mason-Dixon. Under Reconstruction, Kedd enforced the laws with a ruthless intensity that had earned him the enmity of the populace.

O'Brian paused, listening to the music of the hills, the wind's sigh, the rush of a nearby creek hidden beyond the dense foliage of cedar and oak, sweet gum and redbud, leatherwood shrubs and beech ferns.

"And the winner gets to stay," O'Brian added.

Twenty-one years old, he was the last of his kind. All the rest of his mother's people had been relocated west, to Indian territory. But not Blue Elk O'Brian. And so long as he remained, these verdant hills belonged to the Osage.

2

O'Brian reined in the gelding on the creek bank and waited still as a statue in the shade of the surrounding beech trees. No one was supposed to know about the cabin on Tomahawk Creek, but smoke curled from the stone chimney and a hammerhead roan nibbled on the dry grass bundled in the corral.

The Osage Kid was a good two days' ride from where he had routed the Regulators with the bees. Here in this hollow, the Kid had built his humble two-room cabin of white oak and cedar shingles chinked with mud from the creek. The cabin stood a hundred feet from the creek and was all but obscured beneath an overhanging ledge of vine-draped limestone.

The Osage Kid slid from horseback and walked the gelding deeper into the woods, where he ground-tethered the animal in the darker recesses of the forest. Then he drew his Navy Colt .36, checked the loads, nodded satisfied, and holstered the revolver. He opened his saddlebag and pulled out a second Navy

Colt. The weapon's barrel length had been shortened
by a couple of inches, to ensure a more comfortable
fit. The Kid tucked the spare in his gun belt. It fit
neatly in the small of his back, where it rode unno-
ticed. Such a little surprise might mean the difference
between living and dying. During four years of war,
fighting for the Confederacy's lost cause, O'Brian had
learned well the value of a surprise attack.

Stepping away from the horse, the Kid worked his
way back to the creek, where he squatted down and
continued to watch the cabin. As the minutes ticked
away, he waited, studying his cabin and the smoke
trailing from the chimney.

One horse, probably one rider. Probably not a Regulator, since they seldom traveled alone. Then, who?
The Kid sniffed the air. His mouth began to water and
his stomach growled. Someone was cooking his bacon, brewing his coffee. By heavens, enough was
enough! He sprang forward and darted across the
creek, momentarily exposing himself before reaching
the opposite bank. He crouched low and waited for a
gunshot. Nothing happened. Cautiously he parted a
cluster of beech ferns and studied the cabin once
more.

No sign of life save for the chimney smoke, no
movement around the cabin. He searched the length
of the cliff that protected the rear of the cabin. To an
outsider it might appear that the Kid had built his
cabin in a dead end and left himself no way to escape,
the limestone cliff offering a formidable barrier. Only
an experienced eye could discern the series of hand-

and footholds that traversed the face of the bluff.

Thirty yards to the cabin. No problem, the Kid grinned. Child's play, unless whoever was inside had espied his approach, unless whoever was inside shot him through the brisket as he charged.

As the cabin door crashed open, it tore loose from one of its leather hinges and slammed into the faded wood siding of a big old apple barrel set against the wall. The Osage Kid was a blur in the entranceway as he darted inside and crouched behind a table. The interior of the cabin was a dark, warm space intersected by a single beam of sunlight flooding in through the open doorway.

The Kid thumbed the hammer on his Navy Colt and swung the gun sights in an arc to cover a pair of three-legged stools, a ladder-backed rocking chair, then a skillet of bacon set on a rack above the fire in the hearth. The door to the small bedroom stood ajar, revealing a portion of the cot within. The front room was empty. And that meant . . . As the Kid's eyes adjusted to the light, he stood and moved toward the back room, his steps muffled on the hard-packed dirt floor. He scooped up a stool and tossed it at the bedroom door to knock it completely open. He reached the doorway a few seconds after the stool. The Kid crouched low as his eyes ranged across the meager furnishings within: the homemade cot, a leather-sided trunk that had belonged to his father, a lopsided washstand and chipped enamel basin, and there in the dust beneath the cot, Osage beaded shirts and belts, tomahawks and ax heads, tins of coffee, fruit, beans, and milk, all of which he remembered storing in the apple barrel.

Now why would someone have emptied that big old . . .

The Kid spun in the doorway and dropped to the floor, the first shot from his Navy Colt reverberating in the cabin. Splintered wood erupted from the side of the barrel in a shower of fragments as the Colt spoke again and four times more. Gunsmoke clouded the air, the revolver kicked like a wild bronc, the report left the Kid's ears ringing. Every shot struck home, making a sieve of the apple barrel and whoever had concealed themselves within. He charged across the cabin floor, adrenaline pumping every step, grabbed the lid, threw it aside, and gun in hand, peered down into . . .

An empty barrel!

Suckered!

The shutters behind him parted and gunmetal rasped on the wooden sill as the muzzle of a Winchester '66 poked through the opening.

"Never seen a man kill an apple barrel before," a voice gently mocked.

The Kid started to twist around and bring his handgun to bear.

"Don't," the voice snapped.

The breed froze, cursing himself for not checking the perimeter of the cabin. He weighed his options. "What are you carrying?" the Kid asked.

"Winchester Yellowboy," came the reply.

O'Brian was facing the doorway. Across the grassy

field to the fern-carpeted creek bank, an escape route beckoned. All he had to do was break for it, throw a couple of shots over his shoulder to startle his captor.

"Yellowboy, huh," the Osage Kid repeated. "Know how to use it?" Sunlight on the creek beckoned like a beacon of freedom, calling the Kid to safety.

"Use it hell . . . I can make it dance," the voice replied evenly. It was no brag, just a simply stated fact.

"Oh, hell," O'Brian sighed and lowered his gun. He placed it on the floor and turned around, holding his hands up high enough so Yellowboy wouldn't panic and kill him outright. It was a long road to Little Rock and the Osage Kid had been captured before, but never held for long.

"You have done a man's work today, my friend," O'Brian said, turning to face his captor. His features grew slack and a look of surprise flashed over his normally reserved features.

A flaxen-haired teenager stared at him through the window. Sunlight glinted on the brass frame of the carbine in his hands. A boy . . . my God . . . a boy had tricked him, had caught the man who couldn't be caught, the Ghost of the Ozarks, the Osage Kid.

"Awww, shit," O'Brian muttered.

"Howdy," said the youth. He grinned and eased the hammer of his carbine back till it clicked ominously in the stillness.

3

His name was Cole Tyler Anthem, a bounty-hunter, seventeen years old. The Osage Kid stared down at the plate of beans and bacon he held in his chainbound hands and wondered just how in the name of all creation he had managed to let this long-faced youth get the best of him. O'Brian blamed himself. He had pushed too hard to reach Tomahawk Creek and, being tired, he had grown careless. The carelessness had put him in Anthem's chains.

Cole was a tall lanky young man; a shaggy mop of straw-colored hair hung over his ears and down to the base of his neck. He wore faded Confederate-issue trousers and a collarless cotton shirt crisscrossed in the back by his suspenders. A Navy Colt was holstered high at his waist. His Winchester leaned against a wall, within easy reach of his long arms. The brass frame that gave the weapon its nickname of "Yellowboy" gleamed in the firelight. O'Brian noticed the carbine was never out of the youth's reach. He liked that.

He appreciated the trick too, though he wished he hadn't been the object of it. The Osage Kid glanced over at the bullet-riddled barrel and chuckled.

Cole looked up from his plate. "I know my cookin' ain't Delmonico's, but it never made a man giddy before."

"First time for everything," O'Brian said.

Cole shrugged and resumed eating. He paused and gestured toward a wanted poster bearing the Osage Kid's likeness and the sum of three hundred dollars. "I picked that up with a whole passel of other flyers over in Saint Louis. I never had any intention of looking for you. Heck, I was just passin' through and figured to sit out the night in this cabin, but I noticed the Indian gear hanging around and got to wondering about just who might be the owner. Lucky break for me, as I'm down to the last of my folding money."

"Yeah, lucky," O'Brian replied sarcastically, and held up his plate. "How about a little more of my bacon?"

Cole nodded and, walking over to the Indian, forked a few more strips of bacon out onto the man's plate.

"Doesn't seem right. Here we are, two Johnny Rebs," O'Brian said, "now on opposite sides of the fence. And a fence built by Yankee Regulators at that."

"My britches keep my legs warm," Cole said. "They don't stand for anything else. Best you understand that right off." Cole squatted down by the fire. The war that had ended at Appomattox just two years past was a horror he would just as soon forget. Now Cole Anthem was in the process of returning home to the vast and sprawling Anthem ranch. But the road to West Texas was hardly direct. Cole had run away from home to seek adventure and glory, to fight for the Confederate cause. His dreams had ended in failure and a stay in a Union prison. But Cole was damned if he would return a ragged pauper. He intended to make his fortune on his own terms, arrive home a man of pride and substance or not at all.

"You're a mighty young twig to have so much bark on," O'Brian remarked. He set his plate aside. "I didn't give my horse a rubdown when I whistled him in."

"He'll keep for the night," Cole replied, nursing a cup of coffee. He had no intention of stepping out into the darkness with the Osage Kid even if he was manacled.

The Kid sighed and wagged his head and stood. He noticed Anthem's hand drift toward the carbine.

"Easy, Yellowboy, just stretching."

"Reckon we both better turn in so we can get an early start tomorrow," Cole replied.

"Sure, you get plenty of rest. You and I have a long ride, young'un." O'Brian grinned, settling down on the blankets Cole had provided.

"How do you know?" Anthem asked.

"It's a long ride to any place from these old hills," the Osage Kid remarked, the sound of experience in his voice.

Cole looped a rope through the black link chain

connecting the Kid's manacled wrists, then ran the rope around the leg of the table and around his own wrist.

"This Yellowboy and I sleep real light," Cole explained, mustering all the seriousness his long sad features possessed.

"So do I." O'Brian grinned again. He wanted the young bounty-hunter to worry just enough that he wouldn't rest easy. The Indian wanted Anthem good and tired before they reached . . . "Just where are you taking me?"

"Little Rock. The state police will pay on delivery," Cole said. He stretched out near the fire and wrapped a blanket around his shoulders. Either it was getting colder or he was taking fever.

"I don't doubt it. They might even appoint you governor for a day—Major Kedd'll be so happy to get me at the length of a rope."

"The warrant says theft and robbery. They can't hang a man for that," Cole said. He drained the contents of his cup and set it on the floor beside him.

"Not a white man," Blue Elk said.

"Shoot, you ain't hardly darker than me," Cole said. He rose up on his knees and blew out the lamp on the table. Shadows invaded the room, dancing on the walls, fluttering in the firelight.

"Major Andrew Kedd is a proud man. And proud men are dangerous." O'Brian clasped his hands behind his head and stared up at the ceiling. "For two years, Major Kedd's hunted me. For two years I have humiliated him. For this crime, I will hang."

"I'm sorry," the young man by the fire replied.

"Sorry enough to let me go free?"

"No."

O'Brian chuckled. He was starting to like Cole Tyler Anthem and would be sorry to have to kill him.

"April," Cole grumbled, and blew on his hands. He glanced ahead at the Osage Kid, who seemed to shrink in the saddle in an attempt to dodge the brisk north wind that had come howling down the long hills during the night. The air carried the bite of tundra country, a cold that seemed to grow through woolen coats and coarsely woven shirts and made a man's bones stiffen in the saddle.

The two men had been in the saddle for the better part of the morning. Tomahawk Creek lay several miles of narrow twisting trails behind them. The path took them beneath limestone bluffs dotted with the desperate twisted limbs of white cedar clinging to the meager soil. The Osage Kid led the way through a corridor of flowering redbud trees and budding oak and hickory.

O'Brian shifted his weight in the saddle. He began massaging his right leg and managed to successfully mask fitting a hidden knife back into its sheath on the inside of his boot. "The cold makes me cramp up," he called over his shoulder to his young captor.

Cole didn't offer a reply. Instead, he lifted his gaze to study the glowering gray clouds and ruminate over their intentions. If the weather turned any worse, they would have to hole up somewhere. Maybe they'd be lucky, though. No sense expecting the worst. He stared ahead at the series of bluffs and narrow valleys, of the deeply forested terrain that thwarted every effort to follow a direct path from one point to another. Cole wasn't certain they were heading for Little Rock. The best he could do was keep to a southerly course and hope for the best.

"Who'd you ride with?" the Osage Kid called back to Anthem.

"Third Texas Volunteers," Cole said.

"I figured you for a Texan." O'Brian chuckled. "Your family still there?"

Cole started to reply, hesitated. As far as he knew, his father, mother, sister, and twin brother were safe. He hoped the horrors of war had not reached as far as Luminaria, the Anthem ranch in mountainous West Texas. Thoughts of home set his heart to aching. There a man could ride all day and seldom have to alter his course. The mountains were broad and big and windswept, unadorned and barren at first glance but places of subtle, harsh beauty to the eyes of a Texan.

Cole had ridden off to war at fourteen, determined to cover himself with glory, determined to win honor and wealth and return one day as a gallant officer with a purse of stolen Yankee gold and a chest full of medals as tribute to his bravery.

War has a way of teaching a young man the meaning of reality. Three years later, with the war a painful memory, Cole Tyler Anthem was a hunter of men and he had yet to see his first medal. He had never gone home, except in his mind's eye. A chill ran down his back. He pulled up the collar of his coat.

The two men rode in silence, through a landscape muted by the unexpected return of winter. Even the beauty of spring colors seemed dulled by the gloomy cold that had turned an April azure sky gunmetal gray.

The wind in the branches of the hickory made a sighing sound that changed to a keening wail as the wind increased. Save for the shuddering branches, nothing stirred in the wild reaches of the forest. The cold had hounded squirrel and insect into burrow and nest. At least the Osage Kid, riding point, liked to think it was the cold. Yet he could not deny the dread he felt in his mind and heart. Every sense seemed attuned to something grim and foreboding in this stretch of the forest.

In truth, these were feelings he had experienced before over the past few months. O'Brian had tried to pay them no mind and attributed such premonitions to the blood of his Osage mother, a woman closely attuned to the heartbeat of the wilderness. She had instilled in her son a respect for the spirit in every living thing, from lowly fern to mighty bear; the wind had a life of its own, the movement of the sun and the stars were the orchestrations of the Great Spirit. The war had dulled O'Brian's senses, but he hadn't totally changed. And now the Indian blood in his veins warned him that something vengeful and deadly stalked the timbered hills and hidden hollows.

A day passed, then a weary night with neither of the men getting much sleep. They broke camp early and pressed on through the morning and well into the afternoon with the north wind hounding them every time they crossed out from the lee of a protecting hillside.

At dusk of the second day Cole pulled up alongside his prisoner. "Do you know where we are?"

"More so than you," O'Brian said.

"Then find us some place out of this wind," Cole said. The brim of his hat fluttered and the hat itself threatened to blow away until Cole wrapped his bandanna over the crown and tied the kerchief under his chin.

"About a mile up ahead," O'Brian called out, striving to be heard above the siren song of the north wind.

Cole nodded and gestured for the Kid to lead the way.

O'Brian walked his gelding down through the timber to a broad, gravel-strewn creek bed, a winding ribbon of sand and polished stones and a shallow flow of crystal-clear water that mirrored the purple hues of the darkening sky. Between the slopes the air was still and bitter cold, but at least out of the path of the norther, there was some respite to be had.

Half an hour later, the Kid reined his horse to a halt about fifty yards from a limestone overhang well above the flood line, unless there came a sudden downpour, and Cole drew abreast, this time with his carbine in hand. Ahead he could make out a slash in the face of the bluff, which appeared to be a naturally carved chamber, fully thirty feet across.

"It goes back about twenty feet or so," O'Brian

said. "And there's usually plenty of dead wood around." The chains on his manacles rattled as he reached up to rub his jawline and neck.

Cole shifted his weight in the saddle, rubbed his backside, and felt his vertebrae pop and creak with the effort. He was ready to bed down by a fire and black coffee. "What are you waiting for?" In the fading light O'Brian wore a wary expression and Cole inherited the breed's misgivings. The bounty-hunter stared off at the shallow cavern with renewed suspicions. "What is it?" Cole studied the ground around the overhang. "I don't see anything."

"Neither do I," said the Osage Kid. "But I smell something." He wrinkled his nose. "Been a fire recent."

Cole breathed in deep and suddenly noticed the faint aroma of charred wood and . . . more . . . a sick sweetish stench ever so faint yet lingering in the clearing.

"Someone made camp, but they aren't there now. We'd see a fire and smoke." Cole waved the muzzle of his Winchester toward the site. "Maybe if we're lucky they left us firewood." The younger man slapped the barrel of the carbine across the rump of O'Brian's gelding, and once more it took the lead, trotted across the creek, splashed through the icy stream, and climbed the bank to the opening in the limestone. The stench grew stronger. O'Brian shuddered and dismounted. Gingerly he approached the cave, taking small comfort in the knife hidden in his boot. Cole dismounted behind him.

"Ho the camp," he shouted out as O'Brian stepped into the shadows. No answer, no reply, only Cole's voice returned in an echo that seemed weak and leeched of resolve. He followed the Osage Kid into the shadowy recess beneath the limestone bluff and brought up sharply. "See, there's no one here," Cole said.

"Wrong," O'Brian corrected, in a voice thick with revulsion. Cole Anthem froze in midstep, as he saw they had entered a nightmare.

The men were dead. Two men, wearing ragged clothes, deputy badges still dangling from the torn remains of their vests. One man was sprawled across a pile of deadwood, his belly ripped open, his boyish features hidden beneath a mask of dried blood, his eyes frozen in a look of helpless terror. It was impossible to tell the age of the other man. His torso had been broken in a dozen places before being dumped on the campfire, and though his weight had smothered the flames, part of his features had been burned away. The stench was that of burned flesh. Strangely, there was little blood in the cave, only a smeared rust-colored trail from the mouth of the cave to its center. The two men had been dragged inside. But by what? Suddenly the silence was broken by a cry on the wind, faint at first, then louder, borne on the norther.

Human . . . animal . . . ? More chilling than the wind.

"These are your mountains," Cole whispered as the night cry faded. "What the hell was that?"

O'Brian shook his head, then gestured to the corpses. "That mess used to be Casey." He pointed to the boyish one. "The burned fella is Dahlgren, I think. They ride with Sheriff Granbury from time to time, out of Teardrop . . . a town south of here. Don't know what brought 'em out." O'Brian's voice trailed off as the cry sounded again, borne on the cold air . . . an answer in itself, fading, fading, then nothing but the wind.

4

Cole and the Osage Kid carried the bodies of the deputies up above the waterline and piled rocks over them. A campfire of hickory and oak furnished enough smoke to conceal the stench of death. It was well into evening before Cole and the Kid sat down to black coffee, beans and bacon, and crackers.

The shallow cave offered protection from the wind. The floor of the cave was layered with sediment that provided a comfortable spot for a man to turn out his bedroll. In fact, Cole thought to himself, he could have asked for no better place to make camp, if it hadn't been for the dead men.

"You reckon it could have been some kind of bear?" Cole asked, finishing his coffee.

"A bear might have drug those boys into the cave but . . . I don't know," O'Brian replied. "Casey'd been cut pretty deep, with a knife most likely. No, not any kind of bear I can think of uses a knife."

"Well, no man I ever saw could have done such a

job on two full grown men," Cole retorted, settling into his blankets. He rubbed a hand over his weary features.

"Anthem, I reckon there's a whole hell of a lot you haven't seen yet," O'Brian said, grinning despite their sobering campsite.

Cole, who didn't bother to reply, saw no humor in the situation.

Neither man was very hungry, and O'Brian made a show of having no taste for food. He curled around and rolled over on his side, propped his head on his saddle, and soon was breathing deeply and evenly, obviously asleep. At least he hoped to fool his young captor into thinking so. Cole had forgotten to fasten the breed's manacles to something immovable and secure. O'Brian listened as Cole finished his food and set his plate aside. He tensed when the bounty-hunter stood and stepped over his inert "sleeping" form.

Cole continued over to the horses, ground-tethered at the mouth of the cave. He trusted the nervous animals to alert him should anything suspicious approach. Satisfied that the mounts were securely tethered, he returned to the campfire, paying the Osage Kid no mind.

O'Brian continued to inhale slow and steady, knowing that Anthem had to be bone-tired. He heard the rustle of blankets, the scrape of a boot heel gouging a furrow in the earth, the other man softly sigh, the creak of saddle leather. There was nothing for O'Brian to do now, but wait.

An hour. Two. Then, how long? The Osage Kid

woke with a start. Anthem wasn't the only one worn
out. But no matter now. How long had he been
asleep? He peered through slitted eyelids and tried to
gauge the hour and failed. He cautiously turned on his
side and peered at the blanket-shrouded figure lying
on the other side of the smoldering coals.

The campfire had died, and save for the feeble glare
cast by the dying embers, darkness had reclaimed the
cave. Blue Elk O'Brian crawled out from under his
blanket and, kneeling, slid the throwing knife from
his boot. Keeping the chains on his manacles taut to
keep from alerting Anthem, the breed moved with catlike stealth to the side of the sleeping man. The brass-
framed Winchester reflected the dull red glow. The
music of the creek, cold clear water splashed over
polished stones, echoed in the cave. The hammerhead
roan looked up, shook its mane, and snorted.

The Osage Kid touched the knife blade to the blankets.

"I don't want to kill you," he said quietly. "Unlock
these bracelets. It's time for us to part company, my
young friend." O'Brian jabbed the business end of his
dagger into the blankets to hurry Cole along and felt
the fabric give beneath the hard steel blade. In that
instant, he knew he'd been suckered again.

"I wondered if you had a hideout knife," Cole said
from the shadows.

O'Brian dropped his hand toward the carbine. He
froze when he heard the click of a hammer. Cole
moved into the feeble circle of light. O'Brian couldn't

make out the man, only the blunt silhouette of a percussion Colt.

"You any good with that belly gun?" the breed asked. "No, don't tell me. You can make it dance."

"Hell, I'm no damn good at all," Cole said. "But I figure as long as you saw that carbine on the ground you'd figure I was asleep." Anthem wagged the barrel of the revolver. "I'd take that Yellowboy over this Colt any day."

The Osage Kid tensed, ready to drop, grab for the carbine, and take his chance.

"Of course, I'd want to load it first," the bounty-hunter added.

O'Brian felt the tension leave him. No chance at all, he thought to himself. He tossed the knife aside and retreated a couple of steps, scooped up some kindling, and returned to the coals. He fed the embers one twig at a time until he had a merry little fire, and added thicker branches until a blaze flooded the cave with light. Only then did he seem to take notice of the scruffy-cheeked youth squatting opposite him. Anthem's sad-eyed, introspective features split into a grin as he retrieved O'Brian's dagger and slid it into his saddlebag.

"I may have been born at night, but it wasn't last night," Anthem said.

O'Brian scowled and shoved the coffeepot nearer the flames. Water and grounds sloshed within and the Kid decided against walking down to the creek in the black of midnight, chained up and weaponless, unable to defend himself against whatever had killed the two deputies.

O'Brian stretched out by the flames, yawned, and watched the blue enamel pot and the tongues of fire lapping around its fire-blackened base.

"Shame on a man who lets himself be suckered twice," he said, sighing. He looked up as Cole began sliding shells into the Winchester. "You're a smart boy. Then again, maybe you're just lucky."

Cole finished loading the Yellowboy and set it aside. He reached inside his shirt and brought out a water-marked scrap of paper. "I don't care which as long as it keeps up." He unfolded the paper. "I found this map among the possibles of those two we buried."

O'Brian's spirits sagged anew. He was hoping the young Texan would stay lost long enough for him to figure out some kind of escape.

"If the cold holds on, we'll head for the nearest town," Anthem said, pointing to the faded delineations on the paper. "Teardrop. Funny name for a town."

"It's a funny town," O'Brian said.

"You know the place well?" Cole asked.

"Let's just say I'm known there."

Cole shrugged, wondering what exactly the Kid meant. He studied the crudely scrawled map. Someone had marked the creek cave and labeled a few ridges and written in a couple of landmarks to look for. Teardrop was the only town on the map.

What continued to unnerve Cole was the way in

which the men had died. Casey and Dahlgren had been young, solidly built individuals fully able to take care of themselves. But whatever or whoever had killed them, dragged them into the cave, and run off their horses, had handled the two men with ease.

The bounty-hunter helped himself to coffee and sat back against his saddle. The warmth from the fire reflected off the flesh-colored walls of flood-carved stone. The crackling embers noisily obscured any other sound.

Outside, the roan suddenly neighed and pulled against its tethering rope. The gelding reacted in the same instant, whinnying, and trying to pull free. Cole bolted upright, reverie shattered. He reached for his carbine and scrambled toward the horses. The Osage Kid was just a step behind. Cole stood aside and motioned for the Kid to lead the way. "I'd like my guns," O'Brian whispered, peering over the backs of the skittish animals at the moonlit slope and the somber reaches of the trees.

"I'll bet you would." Cole chuckled mirthlessly.

"That's the trouble with you young bucks," O'Brian said. "You never learned to trust." He studied Anthem a moment and realized his argument had no chance of breaching the bounty-hunter's resolve. He sighed and stepped out of the cave. Every muscle tensed, the Kid peered into the night. The creek below glistened like molten silver. An army might have hid in the boulder-strewn bed. The cold washed across his features, seeped through his coat, and chilled him to the bone. A gust of wind rushed the length of the creek bed, found every tunnel and crack in the sentient collection of boulders and bluffs. A chorus of moans and plaintive wails filled the night air.

An explosion startled O'Brian. The carbine spat flame as Cole levered another shell and fired again.

"Damn!" O'Brian shouted, more to still his throbbing heart.

"I saw something back in those trees," Cole blurted out, pointing upstream. O'Brian looked in the direction Anthem indicated. Nothing moved . . . no, there, in the shadows there was something darker still, then it was gone. Soundlessly vanished. As if it had never been. Then again, maybe it hadn't.

"These are old hills. Things happen here that don't happen anywhere else," O'Brian muttered. The silver light faded as a rolling barrier of black clouds obliterated the moon.

"What the hell is out there?" Cole said, shivering, his breath clouding the air.

"Ghosts," O'Brian said, "of the Ponca, the Osage, the Kansa, and the Omaha. This is their home, Yellowboy. You are the stranger here."

"And what about you, half-breed?" Cole retorted.

"I am a stranger everywhere," O'Brian answered. He turned and walked back into the cave, retracing his steps to the campfire. He was grateful for the cheerful blaze and warmed his hands around a cup of steaming coffee. O'Brian didn't want to sleep. He might dream of Teardrop and a girl named Charity Rose and wounds that time had never healed.

The Kid glanced up as Cole returned to fireside and bundled up in his own bedroll.

"I reckon there's nothing to fear of ghosts," Cole grumbled. "If a bunch of dead redskins want to walk the spirit trail, then let 'em." Cole burrowed down beneath his blankets, his features a mask of youthful bravado, determination in his voice.

"Well said," Blue Elk O'Brian wryly observed. "Only one thing wrong." His dark eyes hardened. "Ghosts didn't kill the men we buried." The Osage Kid picked up a rounded stone that bore a rust-colored smear of dried blood. He tossed the stone over to Cole. It landed inches away from the younger man, blood side up. And there it remained, like a warning, throughout the long and sleepless night.

5

Teardrop, Arkansas, was an oasis of civilization in the wild heart of the Ozarks. In the shadow of a towering limestone bluff a cluster of shops and stores vied with the whitewashed homes and humble log cabins for a place along the rolling hillside. Crazy Head Creek cut crossways through the town, dividing the township in half. The more respectable citizens tended to live in the northern half, where the town's bank, hotel, church, and mercantile dominated the smaller but still-legitimate businesses: a barbershop, physician's practice, a blacksmith shop, and the like.

Southtown, as its patrons referred to the lower half of Teardrop, was a thriving if tawdry collection of saloons, gambling parlors, bordellos, and the tents and cabins of farm laborers, sharecroppers, and diamond prospectors who had yet to strike it rich.

"Matt Behan was a widower who struck it rich some years back. He came walking out of the mountains with a sack of diamonds and settled here. He built that handsome two-story house across the creek," O'Brian explained. "When the word spread about his find, well, folks just seemed to swarm to the townsite. Teardrop used to be a sleepy little farming town. Then came the prospectors, swarming over the creeks and caves in the surrounding valleys."

"Do they find any stones of value?" Cole asked, intrigued.

"Just enough to hope for more. Now Behan was smart. He bought land, freighted goods in from Little Rock, married a Louisiana gal to help raise his boys, ran cattle, and raised crops. He prospered right up until the day someone murdered him and tossed him off a cliff," O'Brian said, sitting astride his gelding on the crest of a hill overlooking the valley.

"The Behan brothers, Jordan and Ezra, have about as much use for me as Major Kedd. I heard Ezra's sweet on the schoolmarm, and she's gonna marry him," O'Brian added. "I reckon there's no accounting for women's taste."

It was late in the afternoon and charcoal-colored clouds hid the hilltops and lay like an iron lid over the valley floor. Cole could make out a few people hurrying on horseback away from their storefronts in the town below.

Anthem and O'Brian crossed the bridge and joined the half-dozen other souls bound for perdition and pleasure in Teardrop's more notorious establishments.

"Usually more folks around," the Osage Kid remarked. "Appears they're keeping to their homes."

"We'll find a home too," Cole said. A solitary

snowflake drifted past his nose and settled on his
horse's mane. The bounty-hunter studied the layout of
the town until he found one particular building, rec-
tangular in shape with barred windows dotting the
long back wall. The marshal's office and jail had been
built right on the creek and overlooked the bridge that
led to Southtown, presenting the immediacy of the
law should any miscreants attempt to continue their
sordid celebrations beyond the limits designated by
the city fathers.

It had begun to snow in earnest now, fat wet flakes
that fell with some immediacy and spattered the
horsemen on the slope above town. Cole picked out
a wheel-rutted road that led directly in front of a grand
two-story home that had been erected on the edge of
town. It was a steep-roofed structure with a trio of
gabled windows adorning front and back. Farther
down the path was a one-room schoolhouse surrounded by elms and white oaks. There was an iron
bell suspended from a six-foot-high pole in front of
the school and an area out back cordoned off by a
split-rail fence to contain the youngsters at play. A
kid corral, Cole silently observed. The road wound
down into the center of the valley, curved past a
church sporting its own bell tower and steeple, and
continued on past comfortable-looking homes and ·
cabins before becoming Main Street.

Cole took note of a cabin just out back of the
school. A pretty young woman in a gingham dress
stepped outside into the yard. She started toward the
school, then paused to glance up toward the hill. Even

from a distance Anthem was impressed by the woman's beauty. Her hair hung down her back to her trim waist and flowed like a chestnut-colored water-fall. Her full breasts seemed made to pillow a man's head on a lazy summer day. The woman wrapped herself in a shawl and stepped out on a rock path that led to school, but paused again as if she were having second thoughts about continuing on to school. She looked startled when she noticed the two men on the slope.

"If that's the schoolmarm, I wouldn't mind learning to read again," Cole said, appreciation in his voice.

"Katrina Horn," the Osage Kid said; his tone deepened and a smile lit his features. Then he sighed and shook his head in abject dismay. "Miss Katrina Horn, until she moves up the hill to the house of Behan." He glanced aside and raised his manacled wrists. "Take these off."

"You must think I'm a fool," Cole said, incredulous.

"No, maybe a man of honor," the Kid replied. He sighed. "Perhaps that would be foolish, but . . ." He shook the chains securing him. "I will not ride through town like this."

"You mean past that girl," Cole said, cocking an eyebrow. The branches above were protection from most of the snow, but enough of the wet flakes filtered through to make things plumb uncomfortable. "I don't see as you have any other options except to do as I say."

"I could be dead," O'Brian snapped. "That's the

only way I'll wear these chains into town. Take 'em off and I'll lead you to the cell door."

Cole studied his prisoner. In truth, Cole did not relish having to kill the Kid. Still, the war had been a harsh school and Cole had learned his lessons well. A man made his own destiny, and if he chose to die, so be it. But . . .

Cole brought out a black iron key. Seconds later, the manacles fell away and the Osage Kid was free. Cole made no move toward his Winchester. It was a fool's gambit; then again, maybe he was just curious as to what sort of man O'Brian really was.

The Osage Kid rubbed his wrists and nodded in thanks.

"Don't think I aim to ride all the way to Little Rock, though," he cautioned.

"I'm not worried," Cole replied. "I reckon I've done pretty good so far."

The Osage Kid chuckled in agreement, then he nudged his boot heels against his horse and the gelding started down the slope. Cole and his roan came hurrying after.

Ezra Behan had his rear to the iron stove, a mug of brandy in one hand and his pants in the other. He made no attempt to hide his erection as the schoolmarm reentered the cabin. He grinned at her and bowed, sweeping an imaginary hat before him, the better to call attention to his aroused state.

"Just in time," he said. "I'm glad you hurried. You see, I've been thinking about you. It seems we have

unfinished business." He gulped the last of the brandy
and started toward the brass-frame bed set against the
far wall. Muscles rippled along his wiry frame. His
aroused manhood wobbled like a lance leading the
way.

"Blue Elk O'Brian is here," Katrina said.

Ezra spun around, his passion abruptly diminish-
ing. He grabbed for the Colt revolver on the end table
near the bed and then padded on stocking feet over
to the curtained window. He peered through the glass,
wiped the moisture away, and watched as O'Brian led
the way past the schoolhouse. The Kid paused to stare
toward the cabin. A big-boned youth riding behind
the breed spoke up and O'Brian started forward and
continued on. The riders disappeared around the corner of the schoolhouse. Ezra sighed in relief and ran
a hand through his close-cropped brown hair. A
shadow of stubble shaded his jawline.

"Get me my clothes," he snapped.

"Is he coming here?" Katrina asked. "Ezra, maybe
it's time things were settled," the schoolmarm added,
assuming a motherly tone, though she was only five
years Ezra's senior.

"Just do what I say, goddammit," Ezra peevishly
ordered.

He walked to the center of the room and began to
pace. Katrina brought him his trousers, coat, and
white shirt, which had a ruff of coarse lace down the
front. She dumped them unceremoniously on the oval
throw rug in the center of the room. Ezra dressed
quickly, pulled on his boots, and tucked the Colt in

his waistband. He paid no heed to Katrina's obvious displeasure. If she didn't like his tone of voice, she could just find someone else to marry, not that there was any name as prestigious as Behan for a bride to aspire to. With cockiness born of conceit, Ezra Behan hurried to the door. He pulled on his frock coat as a last gesture of preparation.

"Where are you going?" Katrina asked, worried.

"To get Jordan," Ezra said. "And anyone else I find along the way who can handle a gun." He bolted outside as snowflakes like angry bees swarmed in through the open doorway. Katrina hurried to close the door. She tossed her woolen shawl aside and walked to the vanity at the foot of the bed. She began to brush her hair, wincing as the bristles tore at the tangles. Her bright eyes, like brown buttons, studied the reflection in the mirror. Her full lips parted and she tossed the hairbrush down on the tabletop. The schoolmarm unfastened a few buttons on her bodice and parted the fabric to reveal a thin chemise that barely contained her bosom. The image in the mirror blurred and memories returned: O'Brian naked, standing behind her and reaching past her shoulders to cup her breasts; his fingers teasing her nipples until they hardened like taut pink crowns; and Katrina turning to him, to be swept up into his arms and carried to bed, to the same big brass bed . . .

Snow blanketed the rutted street and hid the false-front facades of the buildings. Yet Cole Tyler Anthem had the distinct sensation of being watched. It made him uneasy and he slid the Yellowboy carbine from its saddle scabbard. As he rested the weapon across the pommel, Anthem's fingers curled around the trigger.

"You reckon anyone's home," he called out to the Kid, riding ahead.

O'Brian danced from side to side and shifted uneasily in the saddle. He felt more like a target than a visitor to town. In fact, the last time he had been to Teardrop, six months ago, the townspeople took it on themselves to chase him out, just because he'd decided to do a little late shopping at the Mercantile, after hours, when Ben Rhodes, the proprietor, was fast asleep. The sheriff had alerted the town, and O'Brian had been forced to vacate the premises and head for the safety of the densely wooded mountains.

"They're home," O'Brian muttered. But the cold wet curtain of snow muffled his voice and the sound of the horses' hooves as the animals plodded the length of Main Street and stopped before the sheriff's office.

The men dismounted and stepped on up under the eaves of the roof and out of the snow. The Kid rapped on the door, but received no response. So he booted the door open and stepped into the chill gloom of the sheriff's office. Cole Anthem crowded in behind him, anxious to be out of the snowfall.

Anthem held his Winchester ready. He suspected a trick.

The room, a typical lawman's office, was furnished with a couple of chairs and a desk littered with papers.

A wall rack held three rifles and a shotgun. Several gun belts dangled from a wooden peg jutting out of the wall. A coat tree stood in one corner of the office, an iron stove dominated the front wall. The windows were shuttered tight.

Cole noticed a row of iron-barred cells off the back office. He nudged O'Brian with the gun barrel.

"Your room is back there. Take your pick," the seventeen-year-old said in a dry deep tone. He sounded much older. "Don't imagine the sheriff will mind."

"Ol' A. C. Granbury'll be tickled to death," O'Brian muttered, shuffling forward. He took four steps; then, figuring Cole was right behind him, he whirled around and swung a powerful left hook. His fist cut emptiness; Cole was still at the front door, well out of reach, his carbine aimed at O'Brian's gut.

"You are just bound and determined to make me kill you." Cole chuckled.

"Shit," O'Brian muttered, and continued on into the back room. He stepped inside the closest cell, closed the door, and plopped down on the cot. He folded his arms across his chest, a disgruntled expression disfiguring his usually good-natured appearance.

Cole opened the firebox on the stove. It hadn't seen a blaze in many a day. After he arranged a few blocks of wood and a handful of timber, he found a box of matches as well as the keys to the jail cells on the top of a three-drawer wooden filing cabinet. Soon he had a fire going there and repeated the process in a second stove back by the jail cells.

Cole paused and peered in at O'Brian. "I'll bring the horses over to the livery. And maybe I can find the sheriff and rustle us up some grub. I'm so hungry my stomach thinks my throat's been cut." The young man grinned, then his smile downturned. O'Brian was ignoring him. Cole looked away, even felt a tinge of regret. He liked O'Brian's spirit. The Kid had lived a wildfire life. Now civilized society demanded that he pay. And Cole Anthem was the instrument of society, of justice. Yet, what justice robbed a people of their homeland and birthright?

Cole willed away such speculation. He was bringing a man in for a reward. It was as simple as that. He crossed the room. Time to see to the horses and find a meal. As Cole flung open the front door, he found himself staring down the muzzle of a shotgun. Half a dozen other rifles and Colt revolvers were cocked simultaneously. The man with the shotgun was as tall as Cole, a few years older with thinning hair and a jaw that looked solid as granite. He sighted down the shotgun.

"How about I blow the top of his head clean off and then we go find the breed?" said Jordan Behan, a sentiment that was echoed by the townsfolk gathering at the front of the sheriff's office. It took no genius to read the fear and hatred in their eyes. A short wiry young man, Ezra Behan, stepped out of the crowd of dark angry faces and passed his brother. Ezra raised his Colt, thumbed the hammer back, and pressed the gun to Anthem's heart and said, "Welcome to Teardrop, you son of a bitch."

6

It was too damned crowded in the sheriff's office to suit Cole Anthem. Time spent in a federal prison during the Civil War had left the bounty-hunter with an intense dislike of confining spaces or crowded rooms, and the office was both. Still, he bore his discomfort in silence because it was a whole sight better than being dead. Ezra Behan was the first to espy the Osage Kid behind bars. He had lowered his gun and ordered those around him to do the same. The men followed Cole back into the office to have a look for themselves at the prisoner.

Seven of Teardrop's leading citizens sat or stood in silence as Anthem recounted how he had stumbled onto O'Brian's hideout and waited for the wily fugitive to return to his lair. Cole told his story simply, without embellishment, and as he spoke, the young Texan studied the townsfolk surrounding him. Steam rose from the cold wet coats of the citizens. A coarse gray ribbon of cigar smoke unraveled in the still air.

Ezra Behan, the younger of the brothers, yet the dominant one, wrinkled his nostrils in disgust. Jordan Behan seemed to be cut from a simpler mold. His hair was thinning, a bit unruly. His clothes, well-tailored, looked slept in. He had square, solid features and a jaw that looked like it had been chipped from granite. Ezra, on the other hand, was a dapper twenty-year-old with a forceful gaze and thick neatly trimmed hair. He radiated a lofty sense of self-worth.

If big Jordan Behan was carved from a mountain, Jeremiah Harlowe, Teardrop's blacksmith, was the mountain itself. He was thick-necked, solid, without a waist, and though he stood just over five and a half feet tall in his boots, there was a sense of purpose and determination about the man that reminded Cole of his own father, who had wrangled an empire out of the brutal West Texas wilderness. Harlowe folded his long arms across his apron-covered chest and stood with his back to the wall, listening and judging the truth.

Reverend Perry Ford stood in the blacksmith's shadow, a man of average height wearing the tense worried expression of one who has been asked too many questions and hasn't enough answers to stem the outflow of people from the area. He fidgeted nervously in the presence of so many men with murder still fresh on their minds. He had joined the gathering at Granbury's office only to act as a voice for reason and control.

"Well done, son," Mason Mitchell exclaimed as Cole's story drew to a close. The cherubic little banker positively beamed. "Now we can rest easy with that murderer behind bars."

Cole glanced up in surprise. "The warrant says O'Brian's a thief and a renegade Indian, but it didn't say anything about murder." The bounty-hunter looked over his shoulder at the solitary figure propped on his cot, his back to the wall. O'Brian was obviously listening but offered nothing in defense of himself.

"Maybe Little Rock wants him for theft, but it's murder here. You just wait until A. C. gets back. This cold ought to hurry him and his deputies along," said the seventh man. The black frock coat he wore further accentuated the pasty white flesh of his face, neck, and wrists. His hair was a mass of silver and a thick silver mustache hid his upper lip and curled over his rounded cheeks. Wire-rim spectacles with round lenses made his eyes appear owlish. "I'm Gage Bannister," he said in a silken voice, and extended a cold, fleshy hand. His attitude was anything but bookish. A red sash circled his thickening belly and the walnut grip of a Navy Colt protruded over the material. He spoke in a disarmingly quiet tone of voice. "I run Southtown," Bannister added matter-of-factly. "What's left of it anyway," His teeth clamped down on the cigar in his mouth, the tip of the cigar glowed as he inhaled then blew another pungent streamer of smoke into the room.

"People will start moving back, now that the Kid has been brought in," Mason Mitchell said. He rubbed the palms of his hands in anticipation of the new accounts.

"A hanging will bring them all back," Ezra said, and he rose from his chair near the fire and walked to the doorway opening onto the cells. "Soon as A. C. gets back, so we can do it proper, you hear that, breed!" Behan's elegant features reddened. His buckskin jacket was spotted where the snowflakes had melted in the warmth of the office.

"For two cents I'd run him up right now," Jordan muttered, his homely face turned toward his brother. "I can get a rope."

"The man deserves a fair trial," Reverend Ford timidly suggested. His hands trembled as he spoke. He fanned the smoke from in front of his face.

"Yeah, like he gave our father," Ezra replied. He swung around and fixed the parson in a murderous stare. "And like he gave Pete McKeil, slit his throat and left him dead just outside the Mercantile—and what about Ulysses? That ol' darkie never hurt a soul. Worked for Pa right through the war. He took my father's death plenty hard."

"And he died the same way," Jordan interjected, his anger fueled by his brother's tirade. "Never seen a man so carved up." The elder of the Behan brothers advanced on the cell. He struck the bars with the butt of his shotgun. "I can see you hating my father. But what did you have against the nigger? Answer me, you bastard, or so help me I'll scatter your guts all over the cell." Jordan looked ready to use his double-barreled shotgun.

"Jordan, no," the reverend called out.

"I want no part of this," banker Mitchell exclaimed, and headed for the front door. He knew the Yankee carpetbaggers running the state held a dim view of vigilante justice.

Cole started out of his chair and reached for the Yellowboy, which was propped against the wall. But a voice stopped him.

"Put the shotgun down," Jeremiah Harlowe growled in a voice as deep as a dry plains well. It cut through the tension-filled air and demanded respect. "O'Brian will have a fair trial. We don't know for sure he's the killer. If he is, he'll have a fair hanging, according to law."

"Answer me," Jordan yelled, trying to ignore the blacksmith. Ezra stood aside, a curious smile on his face. Cole got the impression Ezra wanted his older brother to shoot. But if O'Brian were killed, Jordan would be facing a murder charge.

"Jordan Behan," the blacksmith repeated, "I see you. And so help me God, you bring that man harm and I will personally have you brought before the courts in Little Rock." The blacksmith walked across the room to stand between Ezra and Jordan.

"Murderers are important to you, eh, Jeremiah?" Gage Bannister dryly observed from his seat behind the desk.

"No," said Harlowe. "But justice is." The smith's flint-hard eyes bore into Jordan Behan, who towered over him but had none of the blacksmith's presence. Jeremiah Harlowe, in his plaid shirt, Levi's, and soot-stained apron, carried more dignity and unyielding strength of character than any dozen Behans, Cole thought.

Jordan seemed to collapse. He lowered the shotgun, sighed, glared one last time at the man in the cell, then turned on his heels and stalked out of the room.

Ezra chuckled and nodded to Harlowe. "I guess we can wait for Sheriff Granbury," the younger brother replied, and sauntered out of the office, buttoning his greatcoat as he departed and tugging his hat down low on his forehead.

"Thank the Lord," Reverend Ford muttered. He started to leave.

"I'll go with you, Parson," Bannister spoke out. He slid back in his chair, stood, and crossed around the sheriff's desk. He dropped the stub of his cigar in a nearby spittoon. "Maybe you'll be able to save my soul."

"I'm not, uh, going your way, Mr. Bannister," the good parson sniffed, pulling on his flat-brimmed black hat.

"You will," Gage Bannister, gambler, gunfighter, and procurer, said with a chuckle. "Everyone does." He gave a slight wave of his hand in Cole's direction. "You've a line of credit at the Hondo," Bannister added by way of departure.

Cole relaxed at last, the air already beginning to clear. He opened the chamber of the cast-iron stove and fed another log to the flames.

From the cot in his cell, O'Brian watched as the blacksmith warily approached the bars. He did not know what to expect of Harlowe. The blacksmith leaned against the bars. In his heavy coat the man resembled a small bear. He scratched his head and then used his fingers as a comb for his salt-and-pepper mane.

"That gelding hitched outside," Harlowe said. "It used to be mine until someone broke into my stable and stole the animal. Reckon you're the someone." He ran a hand across his stubble, scratched at his chin, and softly laughed. "Maybe I'll bring him home."

"Give him a bait of oats," O'Brian said. "He's come far."

Harlowe nodded. "Glad you took care of him." He returned to the office and studied Cole Anthem. "You look hungry as a cub that's been too long from its mama bear's teat. S'pose you tag along with me and I'll have my daughter kill an egg." Harlowe stood back and appraised the rawboned young Texan. "Or two or three," he added with a grin.

"Or six," Cole suggested.

The blacksmith headed out the door and motioned for the bounty-hunter to follow.

Cole paused to look in on the man in the cell. "I'll send some food over."

"I'll be here," O'Brian replied. He folded his hands behind his head, leaned back on a battered old pillow, and crossed his legs. He heard the front door open and shut. Now he was alone.

Things were looking up, the Osage Kid thought. He'd been in Teardrop all of an hour and hadn't been hung. Yet.

7

Bacon sliced thick, half a dozen eggs, fresh biscuits hot from the kitchen and dobbed with butter; heaven to a hungry man. And none of it as appealing as Mindy Lou Harlowe.

She was taller than her father. Though Jeremiah was craggy, a man with the bark still on, his daughter was a gentle, quiet seventeen-year-old. She wore tomboyish apparel, faded Levi's that clung to her rounded hips, and a blousy flannel shirt that hid her pert bosom. Her pink cheeks were smudged with flour. Soft-green eyes peered out in guarded glances at Cole as she ladled food onto his plate from a cast-iron skillet. A wealth of auburn ringlets framed her creamy complexion.

"Thank you, ma'am," Cole said. Unruly blond strands curled over his forehead and his blue eyes beamed as she returned with a heavy coffeepot and leaned over his shoulder to fill his coffeecup. "You set a mighty fine table," he added.

She nodded and crossed around to her father. Jeremiah held up his blue enamel cup for a refill. Mindy Lou tilted the spout and poured a measure of the strong black brew into the cup and on his hand, taking care to slosh the steaming liquid over his knuckles. The blacksmith sucked in his breath and gingerly placed the cup on the table.

"Holy Christ, woman," Harlowe exclaimed. Mindy Lou smiled in satisfaction and returned to the wood stove. "Whew-ee," Jeremiah added. "Girl's got a temper like her mama, God rest her soul." He winked at the young man sitting across from him. "She's angry 'cause I brought you home without lettin' her know aforehand." Jeremiah stroked his stubbled chin and sighed. "She lost her ma from the fever, and a brother killed by Yankees at Pea Ridge." He looked around at the neatly arranged room with its orderly clutter of chairs and tables, chromolithographs on the walls, white lace curtains at the windows in the front room looking out onto a whitewashed fence. "Still, we've made a home, I reckon." He patted his knees and shifted his weight in the ladder-back chair.

"A fine home, sir," Cole replied.

The Harlowes lived in a two-story frame house near Crazy Head Creek. The stable and corrals were set back of the house along with a barn and blacksmith shop where Jeremiah plied his trade. Though the Harlowes lived north of the creek, the stables were in easy earshot of Teardrop's more notorious section. Jeremiah welcomed business from both staid citizen and drunken carouser, figuring a dollar in coin or greenback was impervious to social standing.

A winter kitchen dominated the back of the house; the front was divided into a small dining room and a larger sitting room. A narrow flight of stairs led upstairs to three bedrooms, though Mindy Lou used her brother's room to house a quilting frame.

Jeremiah gulped the last of his coffee and rose from the table. "I'll bring some vittles to your prisoner."

"That's my job," Cole said, standing.

"Sure it is. But we haven't had much company lately and by the time you got back your own food would be cold."

"It's not right . . ."

"Listen, son, you'd be doing me a favor," Harlowe said. "No tellin' what Mindy Lou is fixing to dump on me next. I'll be back when my daughter calms down." Before Cole could offer another objection, Jeremiah's daughter emerged from the kitchen with a covered skillet containing eggs, bacon, and biscuits for the Osage Kid. Cole thought he read just a hint of dismay in the woman's expression.

"I'll carry them eats to the half-breed," Jeremiah said.

Was that pleasure in the woman's eyes?

"I feel badly you doing my job," Cole said, grateful in spite of himself. The notion of being alone with Harlowe's pretty daughter appealed to him.

"Your job is to loosen your belt and eat your fill." Jeremiah chuckled. "Mindy Lou, you be sure he cleans his plate. And you could play him something on the guitar. Bet it's been a while since he heard an angel sing."

"Oh, Papa," the auburn beauty complained, her cheeks reddening as her father darted out the back door and headed off toward the stable outlined against the forested slope.

The snow had ceased to fall, but the north wind moaned as it swept between the back of the house and the stable doors. Mindy Lou kept watch, her eyebrows arched and worry lines adding years to her youthful bloom. Tension radiated from her.

"I've been on the trail long and look it, but I don't mean you any harm, ma'am." Cole brushed a hand through his shaggy blond mane.

Mindy Lou glanced aside at him, then realized what he had said and shook her head. "It isn't you, Mr. Anthem," she explained. "It's the town. And what, uh, whatever is out there." An image of the Regulators he had found in the cave returned to mind, and he started to speak, then thought better of it.

Mindy Lou and Cole returned to the dining room, where young Anthem hastily consumed the dinner the girl had prepared. She seemed to take pleasure in his appetite. When Cole had sopped up the last of the egg yolk on a wedge of biscuit and plopped the morsel in his mouth, he stared, surprised, at his empty plate. The young woman only giggled. Cole didn't mind, it was good to hear her laugh.

"Do they all eat like that in Texas?" she asked. "I'm surprised there's any food left in the whole state."

"It's not that my ma never set a proper table, Miss Harlowe, just that I've been on the trail a good while and reckon I left my manners back in the woods," Cole replied apologetically. As he spoke, the Seth Thomas clock over the mantel chimed five o'clock. The hour struck and faded, and in the silence that followed Mindy Lou Harlowe and her rugged-looking guest shifted uncomfortably. Their eyes met, held a moment, then both looked away in embarrassment.

"Come with me. I'll show you something," Mindy Lou suddenly suggested. She stood and headed for the kitchen. "Bring your coat," she said over her shoulder.

Cole hurried across the house to retrieve his coat and arrived in the kitchen just as Mindy Lou shrugged into a coarsely woven wool poncho. She motioned for him to follow her and stepped through the back doorway and out into the dying light of day. A nasty mixture of mud and wet snow clung to their boots as Mindy Lou led her guest to the stable. She reached the heavy panel doors, opened them with ease before Cole could help, and darted inside. Cole came along right on her heels. The chilled north wind was a brutal awakener after the dreamy warmth of the Harlowes' home. The stable wasn't exactly cozy but it was a damn sight better than standing in the wind.

The stable smelled of dried manure and damp hay, of oats and leather, charcoal and horseflesh. From the closest stall, Cole's own hammerhead roan whinnied in recognition as Cole strode down the main aisle. There was a carriage off to the side and a buckboard propped up and minus its front wheels. Cole counted ten stalls in all but only four were occupied and he remembered from his ride down to town that the corral out back was empty too. Near the doors, dominating an area all to themselves, were a forge and bellows, an anvil, a water barrel, and beside it, a box containing the tools of a blacksmith's trade.

Mindy Lou whistled softly and knelt down. Something stirred in the shadows and Cole tensed despite himself, realizing at that moment that both his Colt revolver and Yellowboy carbine were back in the house where he had left them. The creature in the shadows took form. A young white-tailed doe pranced skittishly into the center of the barn and darted toward the woman. The deer stopped as it spied Cole then cautiously approached Mindy Lou, who continued to coax it with her gentle voice. The animal stepped inside the woman's embrace. Mindy Lou scratched the little doe behind the ears. Cole waited a few paces back, not wanting to frighten the animal. The deer stood about three feet tall at the shoulders. From time to time it raised its head, its black nostrils flared as it sought the stranger's scent. Eventually the animal relaxed and enjoyed its visit with the woman. Finally the doe scampered back to its pen, a makeshift arrangement of wire and a couple of boards and plenty of warm hay to nestle.

Watching the blacksmith's daughter, Cole was reminded of his own sister, Rachel, a tomboy, who was younger than he and his twin brother, Billy, by four years. Cole's expression settled into sadness, recalling a time forever lost, a time before the war. How long had he been gone? Three years and then some. Rachel would have grown up by now. He watched as Mindy Lou straightened, brushed the straw from her britches, and studied Cole, her green eyes luminous and appealing beneath her long lashes. She might resemble Rachel but the sensations Cole felt as he drew close were anything but brotherly.

"I call her Baby," Mindy Lou said, turning toward Cole. "I found her caught in a wolf trap, a poor frightened fawn with a broken leg. I set it, brought her home." Mindy Lou shivered and continued on down the aisle of the stable to the rear of the building. It was warmer there thanks to a pair of cast-iron stoves set to either side of the twin doors opening out into the corral. "You see, Mr. Anthem, I wanted something to live. With all the deaths that have driven people away, I wanted to sustain one small life." She opened the firebox on one stove.

"I don't understand," Cole replied, handing her enough split timber to bring the fire within back to a healthy blaze.

"No, you'd have to have lived through the past few months to understand," the woman softly said, more to herself. She looked up at Cole as he passed her the firewood. "Matt Behan was the first, then poor old Ulysses. Then we found Pete McKeil." She walked around the stove and peered out the window. Her breath clouded the glass. "And five prospectors are still missing. They went out to work the creeks and hills and never came back. Southtown is just about closed up except for Gage Bannister's. And Northside businesses too. People are leaving and I can't blame them. They're scared." Harlowe's daughter looked at Cole, who stepped up alongside her. "I'm scared," she added.

It was dark now, night blanketed the window, the moon obscured by an overcast sky.

Cole silently cursed his inability to express himself. Brother Billy would have had all the right words and phrases spilling off the tip of his tongue. Billy Anthem was one for the ladies, the charmer. Not Cole, never Cole Tyler Anthem. Actions spoke louder than words. Yet actions sometimes were inappropriate. Her hand for instance on the window. Suppose he should cover that hand with his to show that he sympathized, that he cared.

Cole inhaled slowly, raised his arm, lifted his hand, and taking courage, lowered it. Closer, take heart, Cole Tyler Anthem. You survived the war, Union prison, a gunfight . . . His hand closed over hers. You can survive whatever you feel in your heart . . . this gentleness you haven't known in a long time.

Mindy Lou stiffened, pulled her hand away, and peered out through the window, a look of alarm on her face. "My God," she blurted out. "See . . . beyond the corral. Something's out there!"

Cole looked past her and studied the night and in the ghostly haze of hidden moonlight saw what appeared to be a man struggling down the slope. The man lunged and staggered forward in blind terror as if it were the devil himself after him.

Maybe it was.

8

Up in the hills above Teardrop, Sheriff A. C. Granbury grabbed for his gun, though he had fired his last bullet the day before. Not that it mattered anymore. A row of empty cartridge loops encircled his broad hips. Granbury burst through a thicket of sweet-gum saplings as a shadowy shape leapt forth from a cluster of vines. The sheriff screamed and threw his revolver at it as he barreled headfirst into the attacker, glanced off, and continued out of control down the slope, losing his footing in the process.

He rolled side over side, choked on muddy snow and a mouthful of fur. He sputtered and laughed at his own panic. His attacker was a white-tailed buck driven down out of the hills by the sudden spring storm.

Granbury scrambled to his feet, espied the wooden rails of the Harlowes's corral a hundred feet away.

"Nothin' but a damn buck," he gasped, sucking in the frozen air as he stumbled down the snow-blanketed slope. He slipped, went down in the muck, rose again, his lungs seared from the frigid air and his desperate exertions. "I'm gonna live," he shouted. "Casey . . . Dahlgren, you hear!" But of course, his deputies had stopped hearing days ago. They were dead. Not A. C. Granbury, though. Never A. C. Granbury.

His breath clouded the air and streamed behind him. Granbury was a burly man, a roughhouser who had never met a man he couldn't whip with bare knuckles or gunplay. Sure, Granbury had known fear before, but never anything like what he had felt for the last couple of days. Granbury had barely escaped with his life the night he and his deputies had camped at Cave Creek. A shape in the darkness, a fluttering shadow among the slopes and hollows, had struck with brutal savagery and killed both Casey and Dahlgren. Granbury had fled, had run like a damn coward, and he was ashamed for it.

The sheriff staggered and fell forward in the mud again. He was within crawling distance of the corral fence, so he crawled. He didn't care how it made him look, he didn't give a damn how he arrived in Teardrop, just so long as he arrived.

Hand over hand, left knee, right knee, God he was tired, a forty-four-year-old man going on eighty. His heart throbbed in his chest but he continued to pull himself along, reaching out to grab a handful of snow-covered earth. At last he touched the bottom rail of the fence and with spirits soaring he pulled himself erect.

"God give me strength," he groaned. He hadn't prayed in a long time. But he resolved to start. He had made it! Across the wide corral, the back door of the stable opened and a man stepped out. He held a lantern in one hand, a pitchfork in the other.

"Here," the sheriff gasped, his voice hoarse. "He . . ." He choked and swallowed and leaned against the fence. Alive, oh, sweet heaven, how good to be alive.

Then something lunged from the blackness behind him, caught hold, growled, and lifted Granbury completely in the air. Granbury even heard his back break, felt it, too, and this time his scream cut through the night, echoing down the dark hills like the cry of a lost soul plunged into hell. His broken torso crashed through the fence, timbers split, shards of wood ripped into him.

The scream cut short, faded, and died as did the sheriff of Teardrop.

"Stay put," Cole ordered in a rough voice as Mindy Lou started for the corral. Images of the deputies lying mutilated in the cave caused him to fear the same fate befalling the blacksmith's daughter.

"I can help," Mindy Lou retorted.

"Stay here," Cole angrily repeated, and ran out of the stable, following the noise of a brief but violent battle and, finally, the sickening sound of bones breaking, wooden rails shattering.

The mud underfoot clung to Cole's boot heels and weighted his steps, slowing his charge. He held the lantern aloft in his left hand and slogged the distance as quickly as he could. The ground hardened in less-trampled spots and his pace quickened. Suddenly, in the perimeter of lantern light, Cole espied the sheriff, faceup, lying on the broken fence. Something was bending over the sheriff's body. If it was a man, then he was huge; he looked to be a head taller than Cole, who was himself larger than most men. Cole could make out black hair and a fur coat or maybe, Christ almighty, a furred torso. The creature's back was turned, its concentration evidently riveted on the sheriff.

Cole's left arm swept forward and the lantern sailed in a lazy arc to shatter on the fence near the sheriff's body. Glass splintered, oil-fed flames consumed the wooden rail fence. The massive man-shaped figure leapt clear off the fiery section of fence and sprinted toward the trees. Cole watched, in helpless wonderment, knowing he could never outrun whatever he had seen. He cursed his own stupidity at having left his guns in the house.

Steps behind him. He whirled about, holding the pitchfork like a spear, but lost his footing in the mud and fell to one knee in the wet snow. Mindy Lou managed to slide to a halt a few feet from the iron tines.

"Dammit, I told you to stay put," Cole angrily barked. Looking past her, Cole noticed Jeremiah emerge from the stable. He had just returned from the jail. The commotion and fire outside had attracted him to the door.

"This is my corral," Harlowe's daughter retorted, outraged by his tone. Then she looked past Cole at the body of A. C. Granbury lying broken and bloody in the lurid light of the flames. "Oh, no!" Mindy Lou gasped, the anger draining out of her. She knelt at the dead man's side while Anthem scooped snow onto the fence to keep the flames from spreading. He averted his eyes as Mindy Lou bent double and retched.

Jeremiah, sensing trouble, crossed the yard at a run. "What in thunder is going on out here . . . Granbury," the blacksmith exclaimed.

Cole forced himself to look at the dead man. The sheriff's skull was crushed above the left temple. From the grotesque position of his body it appeared his spine was snapped. Harlowe knelt at the dead man's side. The sheriff's eyes bulged in a final look of horror that death had fixed. His mouth hung open in a silent scream.

"We heard him screaming," Mindy Lou said. She glanced sheepishly at Cole as if to apologize for her display of weakness. He reached out and patted her arm.

"Forgive me for what I'm about to do. But I got to know," Harlowe softly said.

Cole watched in disgust as the blacksmith worked his callused fingers in the dead man's mouth. Before Cole could comment, the blacksmith straightened. Despite the bitter cold, sweat beaded Jeremiah's forehead, his breathing was labored from his exertions and the distaste he felt for his own conduct. He wiped something off with his kerchief. Harlowe opened his

hand and placed a stone in the center of Cole's outstretched palm. It was the size of the nail on Cole's
little finger and glowed shiny amber by firelight.

"A yellow diamond," Harlowe said. He looked to
his daughter, shivering in the cold. "Daughter . . ."

She nodded, understanding his unspoken instruc-
tion, and headed toward the house.

"I'll fetch the parson," Harlowe said. "I'd appre-
ciate it if you'd stay with my daughter till I get back."

"Yes, sir," Anthem replied. Cole stared down at the
battered remains of the sheriff. Whatever or whoever
had killed the poor man was still out there in the
woods, waiting. Cole's guns were in the house and he
had a feeling he would need them before he rode out
of Teardrop for the last time. It was a frightened town.
He looked down at the dead man. From the looks of
things, the town had many good reasons to be afraid.
And now it had one more.

9

A. C. Granbury died a rich man. No one wanted the yellow diamond found in his cheek, so the townsfolk buried it with the sheriff. Parson Ford read from Creation, from the Psalms, and ended with the New Testament and the raising of Lazarus from the dead. He closed his King James Bible then and looked up at the townsfolk circling the freshly dug grave in the cemetery north of town.

"We've repeated this scene too often in the past six months, buried too many of our neighbors and friends . . ." the reverend continued. He searched the faces of those gathered at the site. There were the Harlowes, father and daughter, both of them appropriately solemn, and Cole Anthem, standing apart from the throng. The young Texan held his Confederate-issue hat in his hands; the expression on his face betrayed his weariness. He was armed now with Colt and Winchester carbine and from time to time he lifted his gaze to the snow-flocked hills as if sensing they were all being watched or studied from a distance by Granbury's killer.

Jordan and Ezra Behan stood on either side of the grave. Their father, along with Granbury and Bannister, had founded Teardrop. The sheriff had been like an uncle to the Behan boys. And if one could translate their grim expressions, Granbury's death was not going to go unavenged. Elizabeth Behan had chosen to avoid the funeral service of her husband's old friend. The minister wondered why.

Abigail Ford, the parson's wife, cleared her throat in an effort to alert her husband that his attention had wandered. She peered at him past the rims of her pince-nez eyeglasses, her mouth drawn tight, worry lines marring what was once a kindly, homespun beauty. The parson looked at her, realized he was still in the middle of the service, and started to speak.

This time the creak of axles interrupted him. The people at the gravesite turned to watch as a procession of wagons wound its way through the center of town.

Granbury's gruesome demise had been the last straw for a number of Teardrop's citizens. The morbid tally sheet was too much for them to ignore. If someone or something was killing the people of the town, then the answer became apparent: leave town and live.

Almost a dozen families in their wagons formed the sad procession. The groaning wheels and plodding cadence of the teams drawing the loaded wagons broke the stillness of a cold April morning. Tree limbs, studded with suckers, bowed from the weight of yesterday's moist, heavy snowfall.

In beauty, despite the gray gloom of the sky, the flocked hills bore their silent witness. Ten more families leaving Teardrop. The town was dying, leaving Reverend Ford to bury the dead.

Cole watched the faces of the Harlowes, the Behan brothers, Mason Mitchell the banker, and the few other families gathered at the gravesite. He recognized what he saw: fear, the blind confusion of men and women under attack, not knowing the nature of their enemy or which direction it might come from.

The wind blew cold here at the cemetery. The iron fence wore a second skin of ice. The glowering sky threatened to lose its temper and weep another downpour of sleet. Now that he had met Mindy Lou Harlowe, Cole Anthem wouldn't mind a delay in Teardrop. As long as it didn't become permanent, he thought, returning his attention to the yawning grave.

"The fools," said Mason Mitchell, seeing in such a departure the shape of things to come; future withdrawals on a bank already stretched to its limit. Pretty soon he would be as like to draw blood out of a turnip as to produce revenue to cover such notes.

"Cowards," Ezra corrected, "who run at the first sign of trouble." He looked at Reverend Ford waiting patiently for the comments to cease. Ezra bridled at the parson's disapproving glare. "Granbury's dead, preacher. He can't hear."

"I know these are desperate times, son," Ford answered. "But that is precisely why we must behave in a Christian manner. We are only as strong as our faith."

"Bullshit," Ezra growled, temper rising. His cheeks were flushed from the cold, a patchwork of veins showed beneath his eyes. He patted the grip of a revolver jutting from his waistband. "This is my faith." He nodded toward his brother. "Brother Jordan's got religion too, a Hawkens fifty caliber. And I'll warrant it'll come in a lot handier than your Bible-thumping. Just ask the other poor bastards you've planted in this boneyard."

Ezra turned on his heel, lost his footing in the freshly turned earth, regained his balance, and kicked at the dirt as if to punish the miscreant earth for embarrassing him. Mud spattered the hem of his frock coat and trouser legs.

"Well, I don't think I ever . . ." Abigail, the parson's wife, whispered, aghast at such outrageous behavior.

Jordan Behan stared after his younger brother, then took a hesitant step down the path leading out of the graveyard. He ran a hand through his thinning hair, pulled his cap on his head, and looked around at the others.

"Don't follow in your younger brother's footsteps," Reverend Ford admonished. "Jordan, his way leads to trouble."

Jordan scratched at his blunt jaw, his mind obviously wrestling with the parson's warning. Ezra was the smarter one, and the leadership of the family had fallen to him now. Such an arrangement made sense to Jordan. He even preferred it that way, since he wanted to be able to roam the hills, to hunt and fish and trap to his heart's content.

"He's my brother," Jordan replied, starting down the path. He offered no more explanation than that. It would have to do.

The Behans' departure seemed to inspire the other mourners. One by one the townsfolk began to drift away, fearfully studying the hills as they filed out of the cemetery toward their carriages and wagons.

The reverend did not try to call them back. Suddenly, he too wanted to be alone with his thoughts, his private terrors, and his God.

"I don't have . . . I don't know what to say," the parson stammered in defeat.

A scrape of metal slicing into earth broke the awkwardness. The few remaining townspeople returned their attention to the grave as Cole Anthem shoveled another blade full of dirt onto the wood coffin. He was only seventeen but he had buried men before. He knew the ritual and what had to be done. Nothing fancy, just a simple labor performed simply.

A blade full of dirt, a spoken phrase of prayer . . . "Our father, who art in heaven, hallowed be thy name . . ."

The Osage Kid lay on his prison cot, fingering the shells around his neck and listening to the timber snap-crackling in the stove. Anthem had left early for the cemetery. O'Brian suspected the young man's intentions. After all Cole hadn't even known Granbury. The sheriff was the authority for an entire county, but he had lived in Teardrop, where he often balanced the demands of his profession with his own desire to pan the creek beds and search the mountains for the mother lode of kimberlite studded with raw gems.

Matt Behan had found his share, as had Granbury, or so it was rumored. Now both men were dead. O'Brian shook his head and ruminated on the advantages of being poor but alive. He glanced at the bars and sighed, acknowledging that being alive also had its limitations: better to be poor, alive, and free.

The door to the office opened and O'Brian tensed. He knew it couldn't be Anthem returning from the burial ground so soon. Then he heard the rustle of a skirt on the wooden floor and caught the scent of rosewater. The Kid relaxed. He knew who it was before she spoke.

"Katrina, welcome," O'Brian said without turning from his cot.

The schoolmarm gave a start, then moved closer to the cell. Curling her fingers around the iron bars, she peered in at the Kid.

"You promised to never come back. You gave me your word," she said angrily.

O'Brian chuckled and rolled over on his side to look at his visitor. "This wasn't exactly my idea," he replied. Her nearness, especially the way her full breasts pressed against the bar, aroused him. He stood and walked toward her, like a hunting cat on the prowl, his gray eyes alert and fixed firm on the object of his desire.

He stopped, inches from the woman. His hands

reached through the bars and caught her, pulled her to his kiss. The woman responded, met his kiss, and arched her spine as O'Brian's hand slid underneath her dark-blue cape and cupped a mound of calico bodice that strained to cover sweet flesh beneath. Lips met and tongues, enticingly searching for each other, found pleasure.

O'Brian paused to catch his breath. "Find a key," he purred, "and we'll continue this."

It was the schoolmarm's turn to laugh. She retreated a couple of steps, tucked a wayward strand of hair into her long chestnut braids. Her emerald eyes flashed with wicked fire. "Now that you're here, I think I'd like you to stay awhile."

"It's a pleasurable notion." O'Brian grinned. "But this cell sort of complicates things."

"On the contrary." Katrina smiled. "It keeps me from jeopardizing my honor."

"Honor, hell," O'Brian said. "We tossed that to the wind years ago." He struck the cell door with the palm of his hand. "Get me out of here, Kat." Urgency crept into his voice. "I don't think you want to see me hang."

Katrina readjusted her bodice, patted the folds of her woolen cape. "Oh, they won't hang you now that A. C.'s dead like Ezra's daddy. Everyone'll know you couldn't be the one doing such terrible things." She helped herself to a cup of coffee from the stove and looked at him from beneath hooded eyelids. Her tongue darted out to play with the rim of the cup, steam drifted up into her nostrils, her eyes made promises she had no intention of keeping.

"Not that you aren't terrible," she teased. She passed the coffee cup through the bars to the prisoner within. O'Brian drank from where her lips had touched and ran his tongue around the inside of the cup, his eyes never leaving hers.

"Bring me the keys. Unlock the door, Katrina," he said softly.

"No," she replied. Katrina's expression brightened. "You'll serve me better right where you are. I'll stay here long enough for Ezra to see me leave. He's awfully jealous. But that's good. He'll quit dragging his feet and marry me." She grimaced and added, "I've waited long enough."

"Yeah, all your life," O'Brian said.

Katrina puckered and blew him a kiss, taunting the imprisoned man.

Before the Osage Kid could respond, the door to the office burst open and Ezra Behan stood in the doorway, framed in the cold gray daylight. His surprise turned to displeasure as he recognized the woman by the cell. "Go home, Katrina," Behan said.

"I just stopped by for . . ." The schoolmarm paused, realizing Ezra was in no mood to listen to her explanation. Hiding her satisfaction, she decided to allow his jealousy to fester, as she fastened her cape and pulled the cowl over her head.

"I'll be seeing you," O'Brian called from the cell.

Katrina Horn paused, brushed aside her braided hair to peer back at her notorious former lover, then continued across the office, her button-top boots clattering on the hardwood floor.

Ezra stood silent, struggling to bring his explosive temper under control. O'Brian knew he did not like being made sport of. Not that the thin skin of Behan's made any difference to the Osage Kid.

"I pity you, Ezra," O'Brian said. "For all your wealth, you can't change things with Katrina. When you see her sleeping with a smile on her face, it's because she's dreaming of me."

Ezra scowled and advanced on the cell, his hand dropping to the Colt tucked in his waistband. "You've talked yourself into a grave, you bastard."

"Last night it was a lynching, today the gun," O'Brian said. "What is it, Ezra? A man of your position can afford to be pleasant. I'm beginning to think you don't like me."

"Shut up," Ezra snapped. He wanted to know what had gone on between Katrina and the half-breed, but he wasn't about to ask. He didn't think he could frighten a man like the Osage Kid; still, it was worth a try. "Must be kind of cramped in there for a man like you, used to walking the hills and riding the skyline." Ezra noticed a roach crawling up one of the iron bars and popped it with a flick of his forefinger. "Maybe we can extend your visit to our town."

Behan's threat struck home. The Osage Kid had paced his cell throughout the night. The eight-by-six-foot space seemed to shrink hour by hour. Yellowboy Anthem anyhow, he was the cause of all this.

"Ezra, you do what you want," O'Brian said. "It's your town, *for now*."

"What the hell do you mean?" Behan frowned.

He gripped the bars of the cell, his knuckles whitening, his voice hoarse and rasping.

"Only that the Behans and the friends of the Behans are being killed off," O'Brian said, returning to his cot. "I wouldn't have your name for a diamond big as my head." O'Brian stretched out on the cot; the ropes beneath the thin mattress tightened and made sharp little cracking sounds as his weight settled on the frame. "No, I don't mind stayin' a spell. Hell, compared to you and Jordan, I have all the time in the world."

"You son of a bitch," Ezra snarled. The veins on his cheeks stood out in stark relief. His eyes widened. His lips curled back in a sneer. "I'll come down here one night and drop you myself." A chunk of wood in the stove split apart with an audible crack. Ezra jumped and sprang around, his hand on the grip of his gun. He cursed and started out of the room. "Mark my words, breed. I meant what I said."

"You won't kill me," O'Brian replied. He spoke with such assuredness that Ezra had to stop and face the man in the cell once again. "Because then we'd both lose."

"What do we lose?" Ezra said. Wind moaning through the cracks in the shutters, the crackling fire, too, were hollow empty sounds, echoes in the office of a dead man.

"Anything happens to me and you lose the one man who can find your father's killer."

10

Gage Bannister cleaned the lenses of his spectacles on a handkerchief then fit the wire rims back on his face. The gambler peered at the woman seated across from him and waited for her to render him her undivided attention. But the widow of Matt Behan was preoccupied with troubles of her own. She stared reflectively at the portrait of her husband that dominated one wall of the study.

"Do you think they noticed our absence at the sheriff's burying?" Bannister asked. His fingers tugged absently at the curled tips of his mustache. His prematurely silver hair hung in thick, unkempt tangles, but his attire was impeccable—a smartly tailored dark clay-colored frock coat, trousers, gold brocaded vest, and shiny black boots.

Elizabeth Behan had discarded her widow's weeds for a snug-fitting dress of burgundy wool that flattered her slender waist and small breasts and hips and swept the floor when she walked. Her black hair was drawn tight in a bun. Hers was a severe sort of beauty, made sharper by the burning ambition that shone in the direct and steady gaze in her brown eyes.

She looked away from the portrait and studied her husband's former partner. "To be honest, I don't really care if we were missed or not." Elizabeth glanced toward the door as it swung open and Gina, the Behan housekeeper and cook, entered bearing a pot of tea and a plate of hot sticky cinnamon rolls. The servant set her burden down on the desk.

"Here's somethin' to put in your tummy, Miz Behan," the plump black woman said. "And I brung sugar and cream 'cause I remembers Mr. Bannister likes his tea thataway."

"Thank you, Gina," Elizabeth replied. "Leave us alone now."

Gina nodded and waddled out of the room, humming softly to herself and trying to conceal her disapproval of the likes of Gage Bannister. The gambler winked at her as she passed. He liked dark-skinned women and had a honey-colored mistress named Journey back in Southtown. Laughing, he reached for a cinnamon roll and wolfed it down as the icing dripped to his knuckles. He licked his fingers clean.

"Why have you come?" Elizabeth asked bluntly. Now that Matt was dead she saw no reason to continue a pretense of friendship with her deceased husband's partner. She had never understood Matt's relationship with the gambler in the first place.

Gage noted the chill in Elizabeth's voice. He had expected as much. "I'm here, dear lady, to tell you that something must be done. Southtown is dying. Most of my girls have left. The house gamblers are playing solitaire. The barkeeps are asleep on their feet, 'cause there ain't enough payin' customers to wake them. I've lost four renters this month alone."

"I can't see how this concerns me," Elizabeth replied. "I often told my husband that Teardrop would be better off if Southtown were razed and the jezebels driven out along with the gamblers and whoremongers like yourself." Elizabeth drew herself erect, crossed her pale, slender hands upon the desktop, and stared at Bannister, a look of complete disdain on her face.

"But Matt never took your suggestion to heart." Gage chuckled. "I'll bet that caused you no end of displeasure." He eased his weight against the back of the high-backed chair and studied the book-lined walls, the fine, plushly appointed furniture, a collection of pewter mugs lined like Greeks in phalanx beneath the portrait of Matt Behan.

"It was the basis for our disagreements," Elizabeth admitted. "He was faithful to you as befits a friend. For the life of me I don't know why. It hardly matters now. You are sadly mistaken if you think such an allegiance has transferred to me." Elizabeth leaned forward so that the gambler wouldn't miss a word. "Southtown is finished. Soon you'll be gone. For the sake of decency I say, 'Good riddance.' " The widow pursed her lips, thought a moment, then nodded, curtly, deciding she had said enough. She reached for a little brass bell on the tea tray. She intended to summon Gina and have the gambler shown to the door.

Elizabeth had only admitted him out of curiosity. To think the gambler had the audacity to come to her with his troubles!

Gage reached out and stole the bell from her grasp. The widow started to protest but he quieted her with an angry glance.

"I'll leave, Mrs. Behan, but not before you've heard me out. I'll spin you a tale of the founding of the town, eight years ago. Listen well, 'cause the ending is somethin' might concern you."

Bannister rose and pocketed the bell. He walked to the bay window, which looked onto the snow-swept hills stretching northward in a jagged upheaval of precipitous bluffs and shadow-blanketed canyons.

Bannister recounted the story exactly as it happened. Oh, Elizabeth knew it well, at least the beginning: how Matt, Pete McKeil, A. C. Granbury, and Gage Bannister had gone to probe the heart of the Ozark wilderness in search of diamonds. They were away only ten days and returned rich men.

"My husband was a lucky man," Elizabeth said. Her lightly rouged lips formed a thin straight line that aged her.

"He made his luck. A smart man always does," Gage replied, his back to the woman. Damn, what a cold bleak day for spring. He watched a mongrel pup digging in the moist snow in search of a morsel of food. He had known many such desperate days in his life. Now, everything he had built was threatened. But *I won't lose without a fight*, Gage thought.

"We came upon a man and boy about five days out—" Gage said.

Once again, Elizabeth interrupted him. Her patience was wearing thin. "Yes, yes, yes, Matt told me," she said testily. "A prospector and his son, both killed by savages. You two buried them, found the diamonds hidden among what few belongings the Indians had left behind. Certainly Matt could have tried to find some next of kin. But in truth chances were slim." Elizabeth turned in her chair to face the gambler. "My husband wasn't perfect. But, then, who is?"

"The names were John King and his son, Luther, thirteen years old. They were alive when we ran into them. Matt and I had been separated from Granbury and McKeil. Matt and I were beat; these damn rivers had never given us so much as a sparkle. And there was John King with a year's worth of panning, a leather pouch of raw stones, gleaming like so many tears."

Gage ambled across the room until he stood before the portrait of Matt Behan. A crystal decanter of brandy and cut-crystal glasses had been left on top of a walnut stand just below the portrait. Bannister helped himself to a drink, raised his glass in salute.

"I can't remember which of us made the first move. It was like we both had the idea at the same time. John King died hard, we emptied our revolvers into him, there on the creek bank. Luther took off for a cave nearby. He fired on us. But when we loaded up and fired back, the whole side of the hill blew up in our faces. That bastard King had stored his blasting powder in there, near as we could figure. The whole side of the mountain came down on the kid. We split the diamonds, set some aside to share with Granbury and McKeil when they showed up. It kept them from asking too many questions."

"You're lying. Leave this house immediately," Elizabeth said, rising from the desk, her face flushed with anger. "How dare you . . ."

The gambler drew a folded piece of paper from the red sash around his waist. He unfolded it and held the document up, out of reach but close enough for the widow's inspection.

"A signed confession, see? You know your husband's hand. And sooner or later you'll find my claim to the hangman's rope among his papers." Gage folded the parchment and returned it to his pocket.

Elizabeth slumped into the chair closest to her.

"So we are bound, you and I," Gage concluded.

"No . . ." Elizabeth countered, running on her emotional reserves. "Matt is dead. And I share no guilt. It is you who must fear for your life, Mr. Bannister. Granted I might have to weather some problems that any revelation might bring."

"More than that." Bannister grinned. "I learned that John King had a brother—a man of some means, in fact, a judge I hear, living in Little Rock. He's searched in vain for a clue to his brother's whereabouts. How long do you think you'd be living in this fine house, wearing that pretty dress if Judge King learned all this was paid for with his brother's blood?" Bannister downed his second glass of brandy. "Now you know,

Mrs. Behan, why my troubles are yours." He filled another glass and brought it to the window. "Matt always drank the best," the gambler commented. He started toward the door of the study, paused to think aloud. "Everything I have is tied up in Southtown. Matt diversified, ventured into property, crops, even running cattle and horses, I hear, down in the flat country. I want you to sell off some of your holdings. I'll need a sizable loan to help tide me over, at least until we can get to the bottom of these killings."

"A loan . . . ? Of all the unmitigated gall," Elizabeth stammered.

Bannister pulled a gold watch and chain from his vest pocket to check the time. He didn't want to wear his welcome out, not this first visit with the widow alone.

"I'll be in touch, Elizabeth," Gage said, and moved to leave. As he stepped into the hall, he collided with Jordan. Elizabeth's eldest son brushed the gambler aside, glanced in at his mother and then back to Bannister.

"What the devil is happening here?" Jordan glowered. His mother appeared distressed. "You been pestering my ma about the money I lost down at the Hondo. You got no call to come around—"

"It was just a social call, Jordan, nothing more," Elizabeth spoke up. "I'm not feeling well. I think it's this sudden cold snap has given me a touch of the grippe." The last thing the widow wanted was to antagonize the gambler, at least until she figured out how to handle him. She had to have time to plan her next move. Damn Bannister to hell, she thought, and smiled and said, "Thank you, Mr. Bannister, for your concern."

Jordan gawked at his mother's remarks. He had seen her talk to the banker or the parson so politely but never the likes of Gage Bannister.

The gambler nodded and made his way down the hall. Gina emerged from the dining room and reached the front door in time to hand the man his hat and heavy overcoat.

The gambler, muttering his thanks, stepped out into the cold daylight. His boots crunched in the snow underfoot and he chose his steps wisely as he made his way to his carriage. Bannister hoisted himself into the seat, relit his cigar, gathered the reins in his hands, but sat for a while staring at the stately house Matt Behan had set on the slope above town, where it rested like a bastion of respectability and power.

"*My* power now," Bannister muttered to the memory of his dead companion. Who knows? he reflected. Perhaps *my* respectability soon. After all, Elizabeth is still too much of a woman to waste pining away. She's going to need a proper husband.

Gage Bannister's grin widened, his teeth clenching his cigar, a streamer of gray smoke curling from between his parted lips.

It promised to be a chilly ride back to the Hondo. But Gage Bannister had his ambitions to keep him warm.

11

Cole Tyler Anthem shifted his weight and stomped his feet, blew in his hands, and stared malevolently at the door to the outhouse.

"A body could freeze to death waiting for you to void your bladder, O'Brian," he complained.

"There once was an old man from Dallas . . ."

"Please don't." Cole scowled.

"The stuff in his gut was like ballast."

"Keep it up and so help me I'll burn down the outhouse with you in it," Anthem threatened.

"A man needs poetry in his soul like a glove needs a hand." The jocular response drifted through the weathered wood. The door to the outhouse opened and O'Brian emerged, blinking, into the cold bleak glare of noon. He fastened his belt and tucked his beaded buckskin shirt into his faded gray trousers.

Cole wore Levi's, a work shirt, and a denim coat. His battered campaign hat was pulled tight down to his ears. The cold wind tugged at the brim. He kept the Osage Kid under careful guard, his carbine at the ready.

"You look nervous, Yellowboy," O'Brian mentioned.

"I'm cold," Cole replied. He was also anxious to be off. The Harlowes had insisted he take a noonday dinner with them.

"This winter storm will play itself out before long," O'Brian observed, breathing deep. He looked longingly at Crazy Head Creek, flowing only twenty yards away. Across the creek, a deer trail angled away from Southtown and past a couple of abandoned cabins on its way toward a densely forested hillside. A fugitive could easily lose his pursuers in such a stand of timber.

"I'd cut you down midcreek," Cole said, guessing the Kid's intentions. He nudged O'Brian with the business end of the Winchester, then gestured toward the rear door of the jail.

"Maybe and then again . . ." O'Brian speculated.

"I've been to one burying this morning. I'm not hankering for another." Cole said.

"Granbury look as bad as those Regulators we found?"

"Almost. If I'd got to him any later, he would have," Cole said. "Why?"

"And you think it was a man?"

"I told you last night, yeah, I reckon it was a man. But bigger than anyone I've ever seen. Why?"

O'Brian shrugged. "Just been thinkin' on it, since I've had the time; it's brought something to mind."

"If you can shed a little light on what the hell is going on, I want to know."

"Why? What's this town mean to you anyway? No, wait, seems I recall that old blacksmith had him a right handsome daughter as I recall . . ." O'Brian nodded, studying the younger man's expression. "That's it." The Kid chuckled. "Welcome to Teardrop, Yellowboy."

Cole grimaced and looked away. He felt he was being baited and had his fill of the game. He stepped back and once again indicated the town jail. "I'm waiting," he said. "And that stew I brought you for lunch is cold as a witch's tit by now."

Taking one last look at the hills and freedom, O'Brian pondered his chances and figured they were poor. But sooner or later the Texan was bound to make a mistake. Everyone did. The Osage Kid turned toward the jail and sauntered back the way he had come.

He dreaded the confines of the cell more than death, but as long as he was alive, there was always a chance. So he took the cell and swallowed the feeling of panic clutching at his heart. He was in a hell of a mess, all because of a moment's carelessness. O'Brian couldn't imagine how things could get any worse.

Then he found out.

Walking obediently to the rear door, he quickened his steps and put a little distance between himself and Anthem. He reached for the door, swung it open, then in a single burst of energy darted inside and slammed the door in Cole's face. The young Texan, taken completely unawares, froze, as the realization hit him that O'Brian was escaping.

"Damn," Cole muttered beneath his breath and charged the door. It was latched from the inside. He had been expecting something far more dramatic, perhaps a lunge for the rifle and a desperate dash toward the timber, anything but what had happened. Cole retreated a couple of yards and leveled his rifle. Wood splintered as the Winchester spat flame. Cole levered the spent cartridge and fired twice more. The door swung ajar on its hinges, the latch completely shattered.

Cole dashed headlong through the doorway, and charged, through the settling dust, into the front office. Gray light and cold wind flooded the room, as the front door rocked to and fro in the gusting breeze. Cole's long-legged frame crossed the office on the run and leapt into the street. The Texan stopped sharply and swung his carbine as he slid to one knee in the muddy street.

The Osage Kid stood at the hitching post a few yards off to the right. He looked disgusted. And rightly so. Three men in the uniform of the state militia, the Regulators, had blocked his escape. And not just any three men but Major Andrew Kedd, big beefy Corporal J. D. Canton, and Private Pepper Fisk. The features of all three men were swollen and ravaged by bee stings.

"I do believe I'll die a happy man," Canton said, gesturing with his revolver. Kedd, his black plume broken and dangling forlornly down over the brim of the hat, turned to cover Anthem.

Cole took in the scenario, saw he had blundered into an already precarious situation, and slowly altered his stance.

"This man is my prisoner. I'm bringing him to the authorities in Little Rock," Cole said, holding his Winchester out to the side.

"Where's Granbury?" Kedd asked, his revolver still centered on the Texan.

"Dead and buried this morning."

"How'd he die?"

"Hard."

The major gave young Anthem a hard look. He did not like Cole's impertinence. However, Kedd was in a forgiving mood; even the welts on his hands and neck and ear hurt less now. His mood had swung from dejection and defeat to elation when the infamous Osage Kid had walked right into his hands.

"Are you a deputy?" the major asked.

"I was bringing in O'Brian for the reward," Cole said. Behind the Regulators he could see a few of the townsfolk coming toward the jail and noticed Mindy Lou among them.

"A bounty-hunter . . . shee-it," Canton said, and spat in the mud. "You want me and Fisk to lock him up, Major?"

"Yes, Corporal," Kedd answered. He ran a smoothing hand across his goatee.

"That man is my prisoner," Cole complained.

"You're wasting your time, Yellowboy," O'Brian

said, hooking his thumbs in his belt. "These Regulators have ears but they don't hear."

"Shut up," Canton said. He pistol-whipped the Indian across the jaw; the gun barrel gouged a furrow in O'Brian's cheek. The Kid staggered then brought his forearm up and blocked a second swipe and landed a haymaker on Canton's chin. A second punch to the big man's rock-hard belly had no effect but a head butt to his face knocked Canton off his feet.

Fisk leaned low in the saddle and with the butt of his rifle delivered a teeth-jarring blow to O'Brian's collarbone. The Kid whirled to grab the private and drag him from the saddle before falling to his knees. Canton was up again and kicked O'Brian in the chest, then raised his revolver, poised to crack the man's skull.

Cole fired then, and the revolver flew out of the corporal's grasp. The big man howled and cradled his numb hand.

Major Kedd spurred his horse forward to shove Cole back onto the porch. The Texan, knocked off balance, lost his grip on his carbine, but he managed to reach out and snare the major's boot. When Cole straightened, he pushed the officer right out of the saddle.

Kedd landed on his plume in the mud. He cursed aloud and staggered to his feet in time to see Cole lunge for the Winchester. Kedd grabbed for his own revolver and fired at the Texan. He fired again and blew away a gout of mud between Cole's outstretched fingers and the carbine.

"Son of a bitch," Kedd roared, furious at the indignities he had suffered during the past few days. He had been stung, nearly frozen, and now dumped in the mud. "Enough is enough, dammit."

"Oh, my hand," Canton moaned, cradling the benumbed appendage, looking like some lumbering ungainly bird with a broken wing.

"I think you fractured my shoulder, you bastard," O'Brian said, sucking in a lung full of cold air as he stood and fixed Pepper Fisk in a steely stare.

"I need a drink," wheezed the private, bracing himself on his rifle, his hands trembling.

Cole sat down on the edge of the porch and watched the major advance on him, gun in hand. The officer's cheeks, beneath a mask of mud, grew livid. His nostrils flared and his breath clouded the air. Mud oozed down his trouser legs and into his black boots. The black plume had broken off from the major's hat and was stuck to the seat of his pants, which were in turn mud-plastered to the officer's buttocks. Kedd looked for all the world like a bedraggled gamecock. His eyes smoldered and twitched as he advanced to stand before the young Texan, gun in hand.

"Son of a bitch!" Kedd gasped again.

"Does this mean I won't get my reward?" Cole asked politely.

12

"Jail?" Jeremiah Harlowe blurted out as he slammed his mug of coffee down on the table. "Who put him there?"

"Major Kedd ... He got in a fight with Kedd's men. Oh, Papa, we've got to do something," Mindy Lou replied. Her eyes were emerald pools mirroring emotions other than worry.

"Regulators ... hum," Jeremiah said, stroking his beard. "With A. C. dead, reckon Andrew Kedd's the onliest authority hereabouts."

"What are you saying?" the young woman exclaimed. "Papa, think of some way to get Cole out."

"Crossing them Regulators makes uncommon poor sense," Jeremiah reminded her.

"Jeremiah Harlowe, so help me I'll never lift a skillet or open an oven door in this house again," Mindy Lou solemnly pronounced.

"On the other hand," the blacksmith hurriedly continued, "we, uh, can't stand by and allow an injustice to occur."

Defying Ezra Behan hadn't worried him. But the Regulators were something entirely different. Then again so was starving. He was afraid of Kedd's militia because in these days of reconstruction they were a law unto themselves. Still, the prospect of eating his own cooking filled him with dread.

"I reckon I never seen a jail yet didn't have a door that swung open as well as shut," he said. His daughter threw her arms around his thick bull neck and kissed his grizzled cheek. Harlowe chuckled and, sitting down at the table again, reached for his coffee. "Just tell me one thing . . ." he added. "I kinder like this young man, I guess because he reminds me of your brother, God rest his soul. But it seems to me you've taken a mighty strong interest in Cole Anthem's behalf, especially since he's only been in town a couple of days."

"Why, I, uh," Mindy Lou stammered, trying to think of an explanation. She pulled off her woolen coat and draped it across a ladder-backed chair. The calico dress she wore rustled as she moved around the table.

"Uh-huh, I figured as much." Harlowe nodded sagely. "Now listen to your papa, Little Bit . . ." The blacksmith cleared his throat, swallowed the last of his coffee, and set the cup aside. "I've seen lads like Cole Anthem before. True, he's got grit and I was proud to break bread with him. There's good in him, sure, and wildness too. But wildness is like a flame.

It's got to burn itself out. Until that happens, he'll be a fiddle-foot . . . inclined to move on."

"I don't know why you're saying this to me," Mindy Lou complained, her defenses up. She brushed an auburn curl away from her eye.

"Why?" Harlowe said. " 'Cause you're all prettied up in your Sunday dress and it's only Thursday."

"Maybe I'm tired of looking like a boy, of pumping bellows and feeding horses and cleaning the stables," the woman blurted out. "Oh!" She stomped her foot in disgust. "Are you or aren't you going to help Cole Tyler Anthem?"

The blacksmith stood and walked out of the room, reappeared in the sitting room, hat in hand, a heavy plaid coat draped over his arm. He pulled it on and buttoned up. He studied his work-hardened hands. They were rough and callused and covered with burn scars. Jeremiah feared his daughter was going to expect too much from the Texan, but maybe that was something she would have to learn on her own.

"I'm gonna see about getting the town council together," he said, then added in disgust, "At least what's left of it. We'll see what we can do for Cole." His expression grew crafty as he finished, "And maybe we can help ourselves in the process."

Mindy Lou nodded. She continued to clear the table until she heard the door shut and the latch fall in place. She looked up and studied her reflection in the mirror hung on the wall near the china cabinet. Auburn hair, green eyes, a downturned, serious mouth, all pieces of a puzzle called Mindy Lou Harlowe.

"What do you want?" she asked softly. She waited a moment, then resumed her work, carrying dishes to the kitchen, ferrying the perishables to the cellar cooler, filling her time with busywork to lessen the pain of a question that continued to echo in her heart.

Jeremiah Harlowe searched the faces of the men gathered around him in the stable. It was midnight, and a bitter wind gusted outside the walls of the stable. Horses in the stalls neighed and scratched nervously at the hard-packed earth unused to the crowd of men at such a late hour.

Old Doc Fletcher perched his reed-thin frame on a hand-hewn wooden bench alongside Judd Priest, the town's leading lawyer—in fact, its only lawyer—who used a barrel for a footstool. Priest sat leaning forward, his elbows resting on his knees, hands clasped beneath his chin, and a judicial expression on his face. The rest of the gathering, the Behan brothers, Gage Bannister, and Mason Mitchell, stood around the blacksmith and waited impatiently for Jeremiah to begin.

"I won't keep you long," Harlowe said, sweeping those around him with an unwavering gaze. "I figured it best to leave the parson out of what I got to say."

"Just get on with it," Ezra said, shifting his stance, his slim hands thrust into his pockets. He was angry at himself for even bothering to come to the meeting. In the end, curiosity had won out over desire—Katrina would have to wait.

"Granbury's dead. Those of you who were so all

fired anxious to hang these killings around the Osage Kid's neck are gonna have to look elsewhere. The killer is still loose and ain't a man here who's safe." Harlowe ended in a dark and ominous tone of voice that caused the others to glance about at the shadowy recesses of the stable.

"Go on," Bannister said; the same notion had been on his mind. "Whoever or whatever's responsible is still loose. I say we track him down."

"That's been tried by better men than us," the lawyer spoke out. "I can follow a legal trail through a whole wall of law books and court decisions but tracking a killer . . ." He shook his head.

"Not a man here could do what you're suggesting, Jeremiah," Doc Fletcher said.

"No, but O'Brian might," Harlowe replied.

"He's in jail, you stupid bastard," Ezra blurted out in disgust.

Jeremiah fixed him in a gaze as hard and smoldering as pounded iron fresh from the forge. "You either speak to me with respect, young man, or I'll drag you outside and dunk your head in the trough and hold it there till you've drunk it dry."

Ezra straightened, started to reply, then shrugged and leaned against the gate to an empty stall.

"We help O'Brian escape and pay him well to do our hunting for us," Jeremiah concluded.

"O'Brian . . . loose? What's to stop him from running back into the hills?" Jordan Behan said. He wanted his father's murderer but not enough to get killed for it.

"Money," Bannister answered.

"O'Brian's no safer than the rest of us," the gambler said. "Hell, chances are the Kid will have to cross our killer's path anyway. He might as well be paid for it." Bannister smiled, silently applauding the blacksmith for his ingenuity.

"Aren't we forgetting Major Kedd?" Judd Priest said. He stood, rubbed his paunch, and winced at a gas pain. Then he tugged at his vest and folded his hands behind his back. He stared at Harlowe, waiting for an answer.

"I can take care of the Regulators and free the Kid," the blacksmith declared.

"How?" the banker asked, but quickly held up his hands in protest. "No, don't tell me. I don't want to know, I don't want any part of it."

"I agree," Judd Priest said. "We can't all be involved."

"But if the Osage Kid were to escape," Doc Fletcher continued with a dry, rasping chuckle, "I feel certain the entire town of Teardrop would be willing to reward him for his efforts in our behalf." Then Fletcher stood and dusted the seat of his pants. "Gentlemen, I suggest we return to our homes. Tonight, there is wisdom in ignorance." He coughed, cleared his throat, and brought a pipe out of his pocket and lit it as he headed for the stable door. The rest of the townspeople followed, save Bannister, who stayed behind to hear Harlowe's plan.

"I lost my reputation years ago," the gambler said with a shrug.

*   *   *

At noon of the following day, the Osage Kid stretched out on his cot and studied the Texan pacing in the next cell. Cole had been walking the perimeter of his confines for the past hour.

"You aren't any nearer to Texas, Yellowboy," O'Brian said in a conciliatory tone.

"No, but I'm warmer," Cole growled. He hated cells even more than the Osage Kid. He had waited out the final days of the Civil War behind bars in a federal incarceration camp. Being jailed by these blue-coated Regulators brought back a lot of unpleasant memories he would have soon forgotten.

"You'd be a lot warmer if you hadn't tried to keep J. D. from splattering my brains," O'Brian dryly observed.

"Don't remind me," Cole said. He paused and peered in through the bars. "It was a temporary lapse of my sanity."

"What are you two mumbling about in there," Pepper Fisk bellowed, walking in from the front office. As soon as he was out of sight of his commanding officer, he reached inside his coat and brought out a round, flat brown glass bottle. He uncorked it, motioned for the prisoners to be quiet, and tilted the bottle to his lips. He drank deep, pouring a fiery cascade of rotgut whiskey down his gullet. Settling on a three-legged stool, he continued to pull on the bottle like a babe at tit.

Before he finished, a look of contentment had spread across his mottled cheeks, and his nose was

cherry-red. Finally, he shoved the bottle down behind
the wood box beside the cast-iron stove, then opening
the firetrap, he fed another couple of split logs to the
flames.

"That thirst was a long time brewing," Fisk sighed.
He opened the collar of his shirt, grimaced, and flexed
the fingers of his right hand, which was still swollen
from the bee stings. "That was a hell of a dirty trick,
you bastard," Fisk said in a surprisingly congenial
tone of voice. He chuckled, shook his head. "Never
did like honey. Ate too much of it once. It was just
after the battle of Pea Ridge. I got sicker'n the hog
that ate the rat." The private shook his head, rubbed
a hand across his face, and belched. He filled a cup
with coffee and slid it through the bars of the Indian's
cell.

"Pepper gets downright sociable after he's had a
few swallows of coffin varnish," O'Brian said. He
rose, took the coffee, and sitting on the edge of his
cot, took a tentative sip of the black bitter liquid. He
stifled a groan as a flash of pain shot through his
shoulder. "Pepper, why don't you look up the doctor
J. D. went to see and bring him over to check this
busted wing of mine."

Fisk held up his hands in a gesture of helplessness
and started to answer when Canton stepped into the
cell area. The corporal's hand was bandaged across
the palm as well as the two fingers, where chunks of
gunmetal had gouged their flesh.

"You aren't gonna need a doctor once we're on the
trail tomorrow," the corporal growled. "Neither are

you," he added, fixing Cole in an iron glare.

Cole met the man's gaze with his own unwavering ice-blue eyes. Though he was only seventeen years old, Cole had cut his teeth on gunmetal, had fought off Apaches alongside his father, endured the horrors of the Civil War, and ridden the bounty trail from Kansas to the Ozarks. If Corporal Canton hoped to intimidate the young Texan, the Regulator was in for a rude awakening.

"I see what you mean about these Regulators," Cole said to the Kid in the adjoining cell. "They're like hemorrhoids," the Texan continued. "Oh, they're not so bad at first, but after a little while they can be a real pain in the ass."

The corporal cursed and started toward the cell, gun in hand. "I'll show you," he growled, then heard the door to the office open. Expecting the major, Canton retreated. He stepped into the front room and found a pleasant surprise: Mindy Lou Harlowe. She closed the front door with a shove of her sweetly curved derriere and walked across the room to the desk to set down the picnic basket she carried.

"Well, what have we here, darlin'?" Canton said as he threw back his broad shoulders and puffed out his chest.

"I thought you might be hungry," the girl explained. She uncovered the basket and set out three pies and an assortment of cold sausage and cheese. She looked about the office, seeing only two men, Fisk and Canton, "Where's your gallant captain?"

"Takin' him a bath at the barber's," Canton said.

"But we're here," Fisk added, stating the obvious. The smaller man hitched his pants up over his pot-belly and hurried to join his partner at the desk. The pies were fresh-baked and the aroma of berries wafted throughout the office.

"Too bad you didn't bring enough for the prisoners." Canton grinned, nudging Private Fisk.

"Men like that are nothing but troublemakers and malcontents," Mindy Lou exclaimed.

"One of 'em is part Osage too," Fisk explained, reaching for a pie.

Mindy Lou handed him a fork and gave another to Canton, who already had a pie of his own.

"You're a sweet little bit." Canton grinned. He scratched at the crescent scar beneath his right eye and then winked at the girl. "You ever come to Little Rock, I'll show you a right good time."

Mindy Lou shyly lowered her gaze, a demure smile on her lips. She tugged at an auburn curl and then pulled the flap of her coat across her calico bodice. "I've never been anywhere but Teardrop. A big town like Little Rock, I'd surely be lost, uh, Captain."

Fisk all but choked on a mouthful of pie. "Honey, those ain't cap'n stripes. Them's . . . ugh!" The private groaned as Canton's big boot ground the smaller man's hapless toes.

"Not to worry, missy." Canton chuckled. "You won't get lost with me to guide you."

"I'd like that," the girl enthusiastically replied. She stood back and watched the two men hungrily devour her pies. "Those berries smelled a mite ripe, so I added extra sugar. I hope they're passable."

"Never tasted nothin' better," Fisk mumbled, his mouth full of crust and blackberries and sugary sweet juice that dribbled down his chin.

"Then Godspeed and a safe ride to Little Rock," Mindy Lou replied.

"Hey, how about us?" O'Brian called out.

"We're starved," Cole added.

Mindy Lou walked to the doorway and, hands on hips, gave the prisoners a look of utter contempt.

"Your kind can rot in perdition," the girl snapped. But if her voice was full of contempt, for all her talk of brimstone, her eyes were merry with a look of absolute devilment. She gathered her skirts, spun about, and hurried away.

"I don't think your girl's gonna be much help," O'Brian whispered.

"Just wait," Cole returned. "And she isn't my girl."

Canton reached out and caught Mindy Lou by the arm. The blacksmith's daughter started to pull away, her temper rising, but she caught herself in time and forced herself to accept the corporal's hand on her.

"What's your hurry, sweet? Maybe you and I could visit awhile, all by ourselves. And I could tell you all about the towns I seen." He grinned, revealing his yellowed teeth. His bushy sideburns glistened in the lamplight, sweat trickled through the silvery growth hiding his ears and cheeks.

"Maybe later, after I fix my papa's dinner," the girl replied. "There's the remains of an old barn down near the bridge. Meet me there at sunset." She pulled free and ran from the office, pausing at the front door to wave to Canton. As soon as she was out of earshot, the corporal slapped his thigh, jumped up, and started to dance.

"Sheee-iitttt, this is my lucky day," Canton exclaimed. He crammed the last of the pie in his mouth, tossed the plate aside, and began to clap his hands and kick up his heels.

Fisk finished his pie and joined in the laughter. "J. D.'s gonna dip his wick, doo-da, doo-da," he sang in an off-key voice. "A captain? Damnation, I reckon I'll promote me to sergeant and get me a gal."

"You wouldn't get a gal if she came branded and hog-tied," Canton scoffed. He propped his beefy frame in a chair by the office stove and watched as Fisk started in on the sausage and bread. Taking a knife from his belt, Fisk trimmed a couple of slices of meat for himself and the corporal. He looked enviously at the third pie. Major Kedd better finish up his bath, Pepper Fisk thought. That pie looked mighty tempting. There was nothing he liked better'n blackberry . . .

Suddenly, Fisk doubled over and clutched at his lower abdomen and let out a moan. He staggered out of the room, past the prisoners in the cells, headed out the back door, and broke into a stiff-legged run for the outhouse.

"What the hell . . . ?" Canton exclaimed, and followed the stricken soldier into the cell area. "Hey, you left the door open, you dumb pissant," the corporal shouted at the retreating figure, who paid him no mind. A chill wind rushed in to replace the warmed air. J. D. Canton shook his head in disgust. He cast an angry glance toward Cole and the Osage Kid. "It'd serve you two right if I just let you freeze," the Regulator grumbled.

"Oh, shit," he moaned. Suddenly, feeling his innards move, he reached out to brace himself and placed his injured right hand on the cast-iron stove.

"Yee-oowww!" he bellowed, jerked away, then bent double again. "My hand . . . Sweet sister's ass, I'm dyin'," he said through gritted teeth. "My gut!"

He too headed for the doorway at a dead run, his hard-sole boots drummed a desperate cadence on the wooden floor. Cole and the Osage Kid watched in amazement, uncertain as to what would happen next. For several minutes neither man spoke. Then O'Brian broke the silence.

"The blacksmith's daughter's pretty as mountain laurel, but her cooking is kind of frightsome," the Kid said, laughing.

The front door to Granbury's office creaked on its hinges as Mindy Lou and Jeremiah Harlowe entered and hurried across to the cells. The blacksmith paused to grab a ring of keys from the desk. He carried a shotgun as well.

Cole studied Mindy Lou with renewed respect. The Texan knew he ought to be talking her out of this, but he didn't relish the prospect of a ride to Little Rock in the company of Kedd's Regulators.

"What was in those pies?" Cole asked.

"Just sugar and blackberries," the woman replied

with a shrug. "And some dock root, aniseed, a dash of snake remedy, madder root, and rhubarb. We use it to purge our horses when they eat something they shouldn't."

A lone, long cry drifted in through the door. A second echoed the first as Canton and Fisk struggled for possession of the outhouse.

"That'd make me swear off eating altogether," Cole replied.

Jeremiah stepped up to the door and tried one key, the wrong one, and tried a second. "Tell me I shouldn't be doing this," he gruffly said.

"No, sir," said Cole. "I'm afraid you might take it to heart."

The blacksmith grunted in amusement as the cell door swung open. Cole glanced at O'Brian, who waited, almost expectantly, anxiety written on his features.

"Let him out too," Cole said, nodding toward O'Brian.

"I aim to. They want you both," Jeremiah said, already fumbling with the lock. A loud click signaled O'Brian's release.

"Who?" O'Brian asked.

"You'll find out," the blacksmith answered. "Unless you'd rather stay here, where it's nice and safe."

"No, thanks, my friend," O'Brian said, and hurried off through the outer office. Stepping around the desk, he reached for his guns and gun belt hung on a peg below the rifle rack. The sharp crack of a shotgun being cocked stopped him in his tracks.

"I ain't your friend yet," Harlowe said. His homely features wrinkled in a smile. "We'll see."

O'Brian wasn't about to argue with the business end of a shotgun. He was out of the cell. That would have to do.

Cole brushed past him and retrieved his Colt, gun belt, and the Winchester '66. As he patted the brass frame, energy seemed to flow from the carbine to the man, and he went from being a lad of seventeen to a manhunter again. He scooped up O'Brian's guns and nodded to Harlowe.

"We're ready. What's the plan?"

"The good citizens of Teardrop have arranged a hiding place nearby for you, till Kedd leaves," the blacksmith explained. He turned to his daughter. "Get along, girl. And take the food with you. As far as Kedd knows, his boys took sick, and these two broke jail and run off with guns and food."

"Maybe I ought to come along," Mindy Lou protested, casting a covetous eye in Cole's direction.

"The Hondo's no place for a proper girl," Jeremiah snapped. "Now go on!"

"All right," Mindy Lou peevishly acquiesced. She led the way out into the street and started on foot toward the Harlowe stables across the street. Jeremiah had pulled a wagon up in front of the jail and ordered the two men to climb into the back and cover themselves with a ground cloth he had provided for concealment. Cole and the Osage Kid lost no time in crawling aboard. The wagon shuddered as Jeremiah took his place behind the reins.

"Bannister's place," O'Brian muttered. He tucked his hands in his armpits for warmth. He had left his coat in the jail and already regretted it. "I wonder what he wants."

"No doubt his motives are purely Christian and un-conditional."

"Yeah, and pigs have wings," O'Brian grumbled. He wrinkled his nostrils. "Whew, Yellowboy, you could use a bath."

"You sure as the devil aren't any nosegay your-self," Cole grumbled.

The wagon wheels rattled on the wooden bridge as Jeremiah crossed the streambed and entered South-town. Both men fell silent, each lost in private spec-ulation on the kindness of a gambler and the generous nature of an entire town, but wondering: What did Teardrop want?

At dusk, the hairy giant sat crouched in a puddle of mud and melting snow on a small promontory above the town and watched, but without real interest. The ways of the town were now as familiar to him as the ways of the game upon which he preyed. The watch had become an unreflecting habit carried out in the same spirit with which he observed the pattern of sun and shadow on a hidden doe's back when his hunger was satisfied and he did not intend to kill her.

His attention was focused within, on the snake that had begun to coil and growl and grow within his belly again.

Luther, for that was the giant's dimly remembered

name, had first noticed the snake years ago in the cave when its power had sustained him in the terror of being alone and still alive. The snake had taught him to take creatures that skittered and crawled across his body in that darkness and use them for food without revulsion, savoring the smoky wetness of their blood, which nourished him. And it was the snake that had led him out of the cave finally, on all fours and nearly blind, to try to exist somehow in the light again.

As he had moved farther from the cave and the stink of humankind, the snake had become quieter, only rousing to flick its tongue or tail in those few brief times that its host recognized as danger. It had slept for so many years that Luther might have forgotten it, but the town and its evil humans recognized from a past become suddenly unobscured had brought it new life. One man in particular had roused the snake to act when he appeared. A man recognized from that terrible day eight years before.

As the snake grew, so did Luther's power and strength. Even as his heart seemed turned more and more to stone, he could feel his body expanding, his muscles bunching and swelling as they filled with the unnatural power.

Luther had not eaten in days and did not know it. The snake and its newfound lust for human destruction filled and satisfied him. His awareness of the mountain and its inhabitants had become sharper than ever, but of himself he took little heed. He listened to the curling and hissing within, which, it seemed, had begun to form speech.

As pale sunlight faded, shadows fell full upon his face. So motionless was he, however, that an uneasy townsman standing by the schoolhouse and scanning the slopes for intruders mistook him for a rock, although he was only partly concealed behind a tatty pine branch. But the setting sun, a milky orb moving through layers of blackened clouds, distracted Luther from the whisperings he sought to understand.

He noticed that a woman had joined the man below. She was one he had watched many times before. Her hair was chestnut and hung to her waist and brought to mind the memory of a woman who had cradled him, cared for him so long ago it was no longer real. The woman by the school wore calico dresses and white aprons and a warm-looking hooded cloak. She lived in a house of three rooms with a deep porch right near the school. Luther had sneaked in to examine the house once after he realized that she belonged to it. The objects and smells, the feel of the cramped spaces that evoked half-remembered images of such intensity that he had panicked and run out, forgetting to replace the tiny scissors he had picked up from a table. And that night the snake had been restless, sending him troubled dreams, disturbing his sleep.

Luther understood that the woman had a name of her own, forever unknown to him. He named her "Mother" and meant to spare her from the blood and death he would bring to others. He wore the tiny scissors on a leather string around his neck, and sometimes, he used them to punch holes in things. He always felt the cold sting of the metal against his chest when Mother appeared in the street.

Night fell quickly. Mother and the townsman disappeared as lights began to twinkle like secrets through the gaps in curtains and shutters. Luther shivered and became aware that the mud in which his feet had been planted for hours was turning to ice again. He stretched and crushed pine needles in his hands, inhaling deeply their pungency. The smell cleaned the town from him and brought him back to the mountain and its complicated rhythms.

"Revenge," whispered the snake, but Luther no longer knew the word, though he lived it. Revenge was a sound from memory, like "mother" or "father" (poor murdered Papa)—noise from another world and a foreign language. And still the snake repeated it again and again, in whisper.

"Revenge."

13

It was a saloon. It was a whorehouse. But Gage Bannister liked to think of the Hondo as the town meeting place.

All the rooms at the Hondo were furnished alike; throw rugs on the hardwood floor, a brass bed, chromolithographs of parks and nubile maidens adorned the walls, two end tables with shaded oil lamps; burgundy curtains cloaked a single window that held views of the street or the alleys on either side of the saloon. The walls of each room were covered with pale-lavender flocked felt that muffled any sounds; the halls were quiet.

O'Brian studied the shifting patterns on the whitewashed ceiling, patterns cast by the flickering flames of the lamps. The shadows had a hypnotic effect on him as he lay on the bedroll spread on the floor. He had propped a couple of pillows against the wall and was stretched out, covered with a single blanket.

Beds, white man's comfort, held little appeal for

O'Brian. Cole had quickly claimed the brass-framed
bed and was already sleeping soundly. O'Brian stole
across the room to stand over the snoring young man.
The Indian could have stolen the Texan's guns and
vanished into the night, but then he would have
missed a meeting with the good people of Teardrop.
He suspected what the residents had in mind and
sensed a profit could be turned. He retraced his steps,
crawled under his blankets, and soon was asleep, with
Cole none the wiser.

"Surprised to see you here," Cole said the next
morning, pulling on his boots. "Deep as I slept, a whole
army could have marched through the room and I
wouldn't have known." He yawned and stretched his
long arms, then scratched his unruly straw-colored
hair. Without making a show of it he checked the loads
in his carbine and revolver.

"I gave it some thought," O'Brian said. "But you
were sleeping so innocentlike . . ."

"Bullshit," Cole interrupted, unable to hide his
good-natured grin. Hearing horses in the street, he
hurried to the window, cautiously parted the curtains,
and peered out at the brief parade below. He waved
O'Brian over. "Look at this."

The Osage Kid crawled out of his bedroll and went
to stand at the window alongside Cole. The Texan
shifted his stance to allow the shorter man to see.
Down the street, three men came riding, through the
chill of the morning, in the bleak light of a newly
risen sun obscured by a brooding cloud cover. Major
Andrew Kedd sat ramrod-straight in the saddle, his

newly cleaned uniform enhancing the aura of military authority and self-pride that emanated from him. Kedd looked to neither left nor right, but kept his eyes riveted to the hills stretching south, the direction several of the townsfolk had last seen the prisoners heading.

Canton and Pepper Fisk had not fared well. They clung to their saddles as if perched atop precipitous peaks. Their grizzled features were pale, their eyes sunken. Lips looked cracked.

Fisk wavered in the saddle and wondered if they could stop for a rest. Canton called him a dumb ass and reminded the private they had ridden all of a hundred yards. Major Kedd then shouted back that he would personally shoot the first man to dismount. He reprimanded both of the jailers and repeated an earlier threat. His voice carried the length of the street. There was only one way for Fisk and Canton to escape the prison stockade in Little Rock, and that was by apprehending the Osage Kid once again.

In a flash O'Brian hurried to bedside, grabbed the carbine, and returned to the window.

"What are you doing?" the Texan asked in a hushed tone. He caught the Winchester by the barrel.

"I'm gonna get the son of a bitch," O'Brian snarled. His features darkened, his expression lost any semblance of a civilized upbringing. He was a savage again. "I'll give him just what he intended for me. Let him die in the street."

"No. The people in this town would wind up paying the price," Cole said as he twisted the carbine out of O'Brian's grasp. The Kid cursed and dived for Cole's revolver dangling in its holster from the brass-rail headboard. The Texan caught O'Brian square in the back and both men fell in a tangle of arms and legs onto the bed.

One of Bannister's ladies chose to make her entrance, balancing a tray crowded with coffee, platters of wheatcakes, and bacon. She was short, blond, and busty and wore a floor-length feathery robe that parted as she walked to tease both men with a glimpse of a satin white thigh. Her cheeks wore a heavy rouge blush, and when she walked, long blond ringlets of her golden hair swung back and forth and lightly slapped the back of her neck.

"If you two boys want to wrestle," she said in a husky tone, "why don't you wrestle with me?"

O'Brian and Cole stared in openmouthed appreciation, then untangled themselves and rolled off the bed. Cole, who was still in his long johns, made a hasty grab for his trousers. O'Brian had slept in his clothes. He brushed his hair back, threw his chest out, and stepped to the woman's side, eager to be of service. His smile was an invitation, his gray eyes almost a command, as he took the tray and set it down on the nearest table.

"I've known that look before," the woman said in a chiding tone.

"But you have never known me before," O'Brian said, his breath brushing her neck.

"And I won't neither," the woman replied good-naturedly. "I'll warrant the two of you couldn't scratch enough together to pay attention," she added, laughing at her own turn of a phrase. The woman ambled toward the door to the hall. "But if you ever do . . ." she said, and this time took in Cole as well as the Kid, "just ask for Dancin' Fingers."

The saloon belle gave a wave of her fingers and started to leave. The perfume of musk and vanilla hung thick in the air.

"Hey," O'Brian called out. The woman peered around at him. "How come they call you Dancin' Fingers?"

"Why, sugar, findin' out will be the best money you ever spent." She vanished from sight, her footsteps muffled by the hall carpet. "Eat fast and hearty," her disembodied voice trailed back. "Gage Bannister and some others want to see you downstairs in an hour."

O'Brian grunted and returned to the window, watching as the three Regulators vanished into the forest. He shrugged and sauntered to the table, where he filled a cup with strong black coffee and a plate with hotcakes. He smothered the cakes in cane syrup and wolfed them down while Cole dressed.

The Texan buckled on his gun belt and seated himself at the table. The coffee burned his throat and was bitter as gall, but it woke him up. The wheatcakes bottomed out his stomach. He felt O'Brian staring at him past the rim of his coffee cup.

Cole met the man's challenging gaze. "Well?" he finally asked.

"Don't ever stand in the way of my guns again," O'Brian warned.

"I'll do what I have to," Cole retorted. He drank his fill, place the enameled cup on the table, and leaned forward on his elbows. "Do you suppose Dancin' Fingers is her Christian name?"

O'Brian had a mouthful of coffee and gagged, choked, sprayed the table as he doubled forward in a spasm of coughing. Finally, when his lungs were clear, he leaned back in his chair. Color slowly returned to his cheeks.

"Your pa didn't whip you enough," he gasped.

"It wasn't for lack of trying." Cole grinned. He could remember a couple of real tannings out by the woodpile. Born with a streak of hellion in him, Cole had earned every snap of the switch, for his father, John Anthem, though hard, was as fair a man as Cole had ever known.

"You ready to find out what the good people of Teardrop want?" Cole asked.

"Hell, I already know." O'Brian grinned.

"What?"

"A savior," said Blue Elk O'Brian, his face in shadow, his tone of voice dry and tinged with irony, the devil's own.

Downstairs, the Hondo was a broad, high-ceilinged saloon lit by two huge wagon-wheel chandeliers sporting oil lamps. Round hardwood tables and curved-back captain's chairs crowded the floor while a massive walnut bar dominated almost the entire east wall. Gilt-

edged mirrors and lithographs of Greek nymphs vied
for the attention of every man who stepped up to the
bar and ordered a drink.

As he descended the stairs, Cole took note of two
bartenders standing idle behind the bar. They both
were of average height, wore brown brocaded vests
over white shirts. One sported a mustache, the other
a full beard. Both men were hard-eyed and looked
capable of handling any rowdy who came through the
front doors.

Another man sat near the cast-iron stove. He sat
slouched in his chair, his legs extended and crossed
at the ankles. His hands rested on the shotgun in his
lap. A broad-brimmed hat hid his features, but
O'Brian recognized the man as Shotgun Ned Price, a
man in Bannister's employ.

A black piano player dozed at his keyboard, his
white hair and beard like snow upon the dark earth
of his features. His head nodded, his chest rose and
fell with every breath. As the two men came down,
the piano player stirred, looked up from the keyboard,
shoved away from the instrument, and headed off toward the kitchen in the rear of the saloon.

Cole inhaled as he caught the scent of frying bacon.
The smell made his mouth water despite the tall stack
of wheatcakes that rode in his belly like a pound of
lead shot.

Gage Bannister was doing more business this
morning than he had in weeks. A dozen of Teardrop's
good citizens were gathered at the tables nearest the
bar, and several of the men were nursing glasses of

bourbon or cups of coffee laced with whiskey to take
the edge off the morning's chill.

O'Brian and Cole recognized Mitchell, the banker,
and Jeremiah Harlowe. A few prospectors were seated
at one table apart from their more prosperous-looking
neighbors. Gathered together were the principal pro-
prietors of the town, a barber, the Behan brothers, and
a local plantation owner who farmed in an adjacent
valley to Teardrop. Doc Fletcher sat with the banker,
sharing a glass of port and waiting for something to
happen. Judd Priest, the lawyer, sat eyeing two of
Bannister's saloon girls who had just emerged from
the kitchen. Dancin' Fingers and a doll-faced, light-
skinned black woman named Journey stood at the foot
of the stairs.

Dancin' Fingers whispered to Journey, whose gaze
traveled the length and breadth of Cole Tyler Anthem.
The seventeen-year-old gulped and touched the brim of
his hat. Journey stood with her hands on her rounded
hips, her small, pointed bosom contained by a scarlet
corsette and lace bodice, a scarlet garter circled her
coffee-colored thighs. She made no move to secure her
dressing gown as it parted.

"I hope you got enough rest, honey," Journey said
softly as Cole crossed in front of her. She started toward the stairs, the hem of her gown brushed Cole's
leg, a hip nudged him as she passed.

Cole gulped. Dancin' Fingers glanced at Gage Bannister to make sure he was watching, then blocked
O'Brian's path.

"I've heard a lot about you," she said, and then,

half-mocking, added, "I wonder if it's all true."

O'Brian reached out, encircled her waist, and pulled the startled woman into him. His mouth covered the woman's in a savage, passionate kiss. When he released his hold, the blond temptress staggered back against the mahogany rail. She blinked at him in amazement.

"Now you know." O'Brian grinned and continued on into the room. He caught Cole staring at him and smiled. "I think I'm in love."

"Which gal?" Cole asked skeptically.

"All of them," O'Brian replied, and continued on through the room, heading straight for the bar, where he helped himself to a cup of coffee. Cole took a seat outside of the circle of townsfolk. He placed the carbine on the table and kept his hand curled around the trigger and resolved to wait for someone to start the party. He didn't have to wait long.

"Well," Gage Bannister began, clearing his throat. He hooked his thumbs in his sash. Lamplight glinted off the lenses in his spectacles and obscured his eyes. His long silver hair was neatly combed, wetted down and parted in the middle. "I believe I can speak for everyone here."

"I want my guns," O'Brian said. He tapped the countertop. "Here, now." He took a sip of coffee, then continued. "I'm nobody's prisoner."

"Oh, come on," Bannister said in his most civil tone.

"My guns," O'Brian insisted.

"Very well," Bannister snapped. He turned to the

bartender closest to him and nodded. The bartender handed him the Osage Kid's guns.

"Hey, I've got a say in this," Cole said, rising. The ominous click of a shotgun being cocked cut short his protestation. The Texan turned his lanky frame toward Bannister's bodyguard, Shotgun Price. Price sat upright now, his hat tilted back to reveal his sober leathery features. The man chewed on a match and leveled the shotgun at the Texan. The bodyguard showed as much emotion as the cast-iron stove next to him.

"By all means, Mr. Anthem, have your say," Gage Bannister called out.

Cole settled back in his chair, much to the relief of everyone in the room. No one wanted to be party to a gunfight, no one wanted to be an accidental target either. Cole eased his hand away from the Yellowboy. He brushed a strand of sandy hair back under his hat.

"I can't think of a thing," Cole lightly replied. It looked like he was three hundred bounty dollars poorer, he thought as O'Brian strapped on his Navy Colt and tucked his other gun in the front of his belt. He checked the loads in his .36 and holstered it.

"Are you satisfied?" Bannister asked.

"Almost," O'Brian said.

"Damn it all," Ezra Behan exclaimed. He slammed his fist down on the table and shot to his feet. "We don't have all day."

"Ezra, we agreed I'd handle this," Bannister reminded his former partner's son.

"Then handle it," Ezra shouted. "The bastard's mocking us. Just look at him."

Bannister turned away from Behan and spoke softly, tersely. "What more do you want?"

"A thousand dollars," O'Brian replied. His answer caused a stir that rippled through the townsfolk seated around the tables. "Five hundred now," O'Brian called out, his voice carrying above the din. "And five hundred when I bring in the killer." He had suspected the reason for his release, and a look at their faces verified it.

"Wait a second. We did cut you loose from the Regulators," Jordan spoke up. "Isn't that a bit high?"

"And I am profoundly grateful. That's why I am only asking for a thousand dollars. I value my life much more than that."

"Maybe we ought to lock you back up," Bannister suggested. At a glance from their employer, the two bartenders brought out a pair of Colt revolvers from behind the bar. O'Brian was covered before his hand moved an inch toward his gun.

O'Brian shrugged. "Sure, lock me up. Jail's the safest place to be in this town. I sleep easy surrounded by iron bars." The Kid leaned with his spine against the bar, his elbows braced on the polished walnut surface. "No one knows these hills better than me," he continued, his dark eyes ranging across the room. Fear and desperation hung in the air—an Osage could smell it in a man. "Go ahead. Lock me up. Tomorrow's Sunday. A new week begins. How many will die in the next seven days? How many more will leave? How much more of the town will die? A thousand dollars is cheap. And look at it this way: if I get killed, you won't have to pay the other five hundred."

"You're robbing us blind," Mason Mitchell sputtered in a blustery voice.

Old Doc Fletcher placed a hand on the banker's arm. "Oh, hell, he's been doing that for years now. So what else is new? Calm down, Mason, calm down."

The banker's cheeks reddened, but his sense of outrage cooled and he sat down.

"I don't like this any more than the rest of you," Gage Bannister said, studying the townsmen. "But I don't see anybody volunteering to take Granbury's place to try to track down this butchering madman, whoever he is." Bannister stared at prospectors, who couldn't meet his gaze, and the notables of the town bundled in their frock coats and struggling, each man in his own way, with his lack of courage.

"Oh, hell, I'll go," Cole spoke out. Bannister and the Osage Kid glanced up in surprise. Mitchell, Doc, Harlowe, and the rest craned their heads around to stare at the young bounty-hunter in surprise.

"You ain't been shaving long enough, son," one of the prospectors spoke out. "This is a man-sized job."

Several of the townsfolk nodded in accord.

"I brought in the Osage Kid," Cole angrily reminded them. He stood, towering over the gathering, carbine in hand. He caught a motion out of the corner of his eye and swung toward Bannister's peacekeeper by the stove, who brought the scattergun to bear.

"Go ahead," Cole said in a murderous tone. "Start

the dance. But before I go down, I'll waltz a forty-four slug right between your eyes."

Bannister's man was caught by surprise. He hadn't expected defiance. His eyes grew wide and he glanced toward the Hondo's owner for support, but he couldn't read Bannister, so he did the next best thing. He lowered the shotgun. Cole looked back at the men around the table.

"You don't have to pay me a thing. But if my bullet brings down your sheriff's killer, then you'll owe me a thousand dollars." He stood, staring at the group, waiting for a reply.

"I guess two hunters are better than one," Bannister finally conceded. He looked at O'Brian. "You don't do the killing, you lose the other five hundred."

O'Brian agreed, reluctantly.

"Then it's settled," Mason Mitchell exclaimed, his voice light, almost cheery. "C'mon, Doc, the wife's fixing ham and eggs."

A rasp of chair legs on the hardwood floor, the murmur of last-minute conversation. A euphoric aura seemed to fill the saloon as if the killer stalking the surrounding hills had already been brought to justice.

Cole looked up as Jeremiah Harlowe stood in front of him, displeasure plain to see. The blacksmith placed a callused hand on the Texan. "Me and Mindy Lou didn't get you out of that pokey just so you could put yourself in line to have your throat slit." The blacksmith's homely honest features mellowed as his eyes searched those of the younger man. "You forgettin' Granbury, lad?"

"No, Mr. Harlowe," Cole said. "And I'm not forgetting Mindy either." He braced the carbine on the tabletop and leaned toward the blacksmith. "What happened to the sheriff and those others you spoke of could have been your daughter. Or you." Cole straightened. "Someone's got to stop it. Anyway, it's the least I can do to repay you for lettin' me take your daughter to the church social tomorrow night."

"You're a bodacious rascal." Jeremiah chuckled and wagged his head. He grabbed Cole by the arm and gently steered him toward the door. "C'mon. I better bring you home. These pictures of naked wommen Bannister's got hung up around here might light a fire that you expect Mindy Lou to put out. It'd pain me to pin your ears back."

"I'd find it a bother myself," Cole said. He glanced at O'Brian, who raised a shot glass in salute.

The Kid looked as if he'd won a prize. Some prize, Cole considered ruefully, one he too had put himself in line to collect.

14

Luther sat beneath a lightning-twisted pine. It was still
afternoon, but the ravaged remnants of the tree protected him from discovery. He preferred to stay farther back, where the heavily wooded ridge provided
adequate concealment, but the snake in his belly had
driven him down, insisting he return to the town. The
snake was hungry, but it would have to wait. Just like
Luther had waited. He had heard the church bells
pealing out across the melting snow. Now he watched
as families in wagon and carriage, on foot or
horseback, moved through Teardrop to the northern-
most edge of town.

Luther, who recognized Katrina as she arrived in a
carriage with Ezra Behan, smiled and whispered the
word "Mother." He watched children running about
and felt an ache rise in his chest that was almost un-
bearable. Others came filing past, but provoked no
reaction. Then at last he saw a surrey carrying five
people from Southtown. There were two fancy

women Luther did not know, but the Indian made an impression. Something about the Osage troubled Luther. When Shotgun, the Hondo's peacekeeper, climbed out of the carriage, Luther's expression remained unchanged, but then Gage Bannister stepped down into the wind.

The snake coiled and bared its fangs. It knew this one with the round glass eyes and so did Luther. Hatred coursed through him. This was the last of the men who had come to steal the pretty stones, who had killed the father and buried the son alive in the cave.

Bannister pulled the collar of his long gray coat up around his ears and neck and headed for the Congregational church, where the annual spring social was being held. As he paused to study the surrounding hills, he stared right at Luther, who remained motionless. The giant's matted beard and hair and his hide-covered body blended into the backdrop of the muddy slope. Bannister shrugged uneasily, but saw nothing. He continued on up the stairs and followed the tinkling music from Abigail's piano inside.

Luther settled back against a twisted limb. Be patient, said the snake. Luther shaded his eyes and located the house by the school. It was empty now and waiting for him. Maybe he could find something more of the woman's to keep with him, to bring to his cave in the hills, something of Mother.

But darkness must come first before he entered the town. Though the ground was moist and chilled him, he ignored the discomfort. He had borne worse. To-night the snake would strike down the glass-eyed man and maybe the snake would be satisfied.

Parson Perry Ford's benevolent gaze swept the room, and a smile came to his face. People actually seemed happy. And it was Abigail's doing, really. She had insisted the event come off as planned despite the terrible tragedies that had so plagued Teardrop. "People need to know life goes on" and "We must refuse to surrender the quality of our lives here to fear," were two of her favorite arguments.

So the pews had been moved aside and the walls and pulpit decorated with paper lace and purple phlox that Abigail had picked before the snowfall and kept alive in every available container of water the parsonage had to offer. There were children underfoot, prospectors and their wives gathered at the long boards to sample a delicious variety of pies and loaf cakes, sweet preserves and fry bread, sugar-cured hams sliced thick on the platter, and Abigail's own specialty, sweet-potato casseroles.

Many of the townsmen had led their wives to the center of the room to dance the slow three-step Abigail was playing.

The parson waved to a tall lad of thirteen who hurried to the preacher's side.

"Tommy, check the lamps for me and give them some wick, the shadows are beginning to fall," the reverend said.

Tommy Mitchell, the banker's son, darted away to

undertake his important mission. As he cut through the dancers, he caromed off Cole Anthem and left a "Sorry, sir" in his wake.

Cole laughed, tightened his hold on the girl in his arms, and resumed dancing by stepping on Mindy's toes. She yelped and pulled away as Cole reddened.

"I guess I dance about as good as a grizzly quilts," he said.

"Just follow me," Mindy Lou replied.

"I thought I was supposed to lead," Cole protested.

"The one who knows the way leads," the young woman explained.

"Oh." Cole wasn't proud. He would give this gal full rein as long as he could keep her in his arms. He toyed with some other notions that made him look around for Jeremiah Harlowe in alarm. The old mind reader had had to repair a broken axle on Doc Fletcher's carriage and evidently was still at the stable.

Cole began his count again and tried to concentrate on keeping his steps in time with Abigail's music as the banker and his agitated wife cut in front of them.

"I can't get over the nerve," Mrs. Mitchell was saying, and she gestured with her fan toward Bannister's women. "Allowing those common trollops to come."

"Now, now, my dear," Mason Mitchell soothed as they moved away from the younger couple.

Cole glanced around and caught the attention of O'Brian. The Osage winked at the bounty-hunter, then he bent down and kissed the girl whose name he had shortened to Dancin'. Bannister's girls were impossible to overlook. Most of the townswomen wore dresses of homespun cotton or heavy wool and appeared the soul of propriety, Journey and Dancin' wore gaudy outfits of feather boas and silken dresses in fuchsia and lime green. To make matters worse, Dancin' was openly friendly and greeted those around her as if they were good friends, especially the husbands, which only made the wives more uncomfortable.

Bannister stood at the corner of a makeshift table, enjoying the discomfort his presence aroused. His frock coat hung open and sweat trickled down his round red cheeks and stained his silk shirt. His glasses gleamed in refracted candlelight as he ate, littering his beard with crumbs. He had started on his third sandwich of ham and buttered bread. Journey kept close to him, her eyes downcast. Her breasts threatened to escape her low-cut bodice, and she was ashamed to be in a church wearing such attire.

Bannister had ordered her to come, and he was not a man to refuse.

Shotgun Price, the gambler's bodyguard, had left his scattergun behind in the surrey. He sat slouched in a corner, his spare frame close to the stove as he sucked on a pocket flask of whiskey. Folks left him alone. He was mean and rode a quick temper as unpredictable as a wild bronc. Men called him Shotgun not only for the weapon he carried but because of the man's dangerous nature. All afternoon, into evening, his mean little eyes had remained fixed on the Texan, whom he hated. For Cole had backed him down. Shotgun had replayed the moment in his mind again and again, as if by changing the outcome in his thoughts it would alter what had actually occurred. It didn't, of course. And the more it bothered him, the more he drank, until the flat, glass bottle was empty.

Cole stumbled his way through to the end of the dance and led Mindy Lou off to the side of the church. There he sat stiffly, chafing in the frock coat and high-collared shirt Jeremiah had loaned him from a trunk of clothes that once belonged to the blacksmith's son. Anthem's broad shoulders strained the fabric of the coat and he had to carefully gauge his movements. His hair hung long and straight, and he had shaved till his skin burned in order to be a proper escort for Harlowe's daughter.

Mindy Lou was easy to be with, he thought. And he felt drawn to her. There had been no room in his life for tenderness, until now, and here he was, needing her gentleness. It had happened swiftly, surely. He hoped that maybe, in some unexplainable way, Mindy Lou needed him.

"What are you thinking, Cole Tyler Anthem?" the young woman asked. She wore a simple dark-blue dress with a pale-blue pinafore, and her auburn hair hung down in ringlets. He thought she looked as pretty as a wildflower.

"I was just trying to figure how many?" Cole grinned.

"How many what?"

"Freckles on your nose," Cole said in a serious tone.

"Oh, you . . . !" She giggled and leaned into him to

pinch his side. She smelled of rose and peppermint, her arm was warm and soft. He caught her hand and held it. A middle-aged woman sitting nearby tilted her head down and peered at him over the rim of her pince-nez, disapproval etched plainly on her features. Cole widened his eyes and bared his teeth. The woman gasped and looked away, her brown woolen dress rustling as she slid farther down the pew, distancing herself from the young couple. Her husband, a local planter, returned with a plate full of food.

"Things are coming to a pretty turn," the woman said. "Why doesn't Mr. Mitchell order the likes of Gage Bannister and the half-breed and some others to leave? The social is for decent folks."

"Because Bannister's money started the bank," her husband said. He looked at Cole and then the Osage Kid, who was standing at the buffet table. "As for the others, Mitchell doesn't want to get himself killed. And neither do I." The planter's wife started to reply. "Eat," her husband snapped, ending the discussion.

"I'm hungry," Mindy Lou announced. She glanced toward the table and saw there was still plenty of food left, even though many of the families had eaten and left, eager to be home before dark.

Cole noticed Shotgun sitting near the table and groaned. Anthem wasn't looking for trouble, but from the look of Bannister's man . . .

Mindy Lou thought Cole was staring at Dancin' and Journey in their feathery finery. Was one of them the object of Cole's interest? "Just how did you pass the time that night you spent at the Hondo, Mr. Anthem?" she asked.

Abigail Ford rescued the Texan from his innocent embarrassment. She approached the young couple and put her arm around Mindy Lou's shoulders. Cole expected another deprecatory aside, but the parson's wife surprised him. Her plain and pedestrian features were transformed by an honest smile.

"Mr. Anthem, is it? My, you two made quite a handsome couple during that three-step," she said.

"Miss Harlowe is gracious to put up with my efforts," Cole replied, reappraising the woman.

"Nonsense," Abigail said. She patted Cole's arm. "You're doing fine. Anyway, learning to dance is half the fun." The older woman lowered her voice and continued in a conspiratorial tone. "You get to squeeze your partner a whole lot tighter."

"Mrs. Ford . . . !" Mindy Lou exclaimed, her astonishment a trifle forced.

Abigail straightened and laughed softly as she smoothed the wrinkles from her charcoal-gray skirt. The lace trim at her wrists and neck had yellowed since first she had worn the dress six years ago. It had been an anniversary present that the parson had managed to buy by setting aside a portion of his meager earnings for a full year.

"Don't you act so surprised, Mindy Harlowe," Abigail said. "After all, that was how I captured Parson Ford. I let him put his arms around me and hold me tight while I showed him how to dance. Next thing I knew, I was a preacher's wife."

"Oh, now I understand," Cole said, enjoying himself.

Mindy Lou's features had turned quite red. And there was no escape though she tried to will away the blush from her cheeks. "I'm hungry," Mindy repeated in a desperate bid to change the subject.

"I'll bet you are," Cole said.

"I baked an egg custard you simply have to taste to believe," Abigail said. "Flavored it with molasses and just a touch of cinnamon. You must try it." She noticed another couple preparing to leave. "That is, if Jordan left any. He loves an egg custard." She turned and went back to the piano, where she started to play a Virginia reel. Conversation subsided as couples returned to the center of the church floor. The town barber and his wife paused by their coats and decided to delay their departure. It was far more cheerful being in the church among friends than in their small rooms above his shop.

Mindy tugged on Cole's sleeve, eager to join the other dancers. Katrina and Ezra whirled past. And Gage Bannister with Dancin', who made no effort to hide her enjoyment. Other townsmen and their wives began spinning about and kicking up their heels in fine fashion.

"I don't know," Cole balked. The last dance had been a lot slower. "I thought you wanted to eat."

"I can wait," Mindy replied. "C'mon, Mr. Anthem, this can't be any harder than fighting Yankees."

Cole started to explain that he was only supposed to kill Yankees, not marry them. But he decided to leave well enough alone and followed Mindy Lou into the fray.

Darkness was Luther's friend. Night always reminded him of the cave, of the night the snake first spoke and told him to ignore his bruised head, to ignore the pain and the fear, the terror, and taught him to live.

Luther grew to manhood among the solitary hills. He set traps for fresh meat, prowled the mountains, keeping away from pockets of civilization, settlements and towns, confining his nocturnal raids to an occasional farm, isolated cabin, or a brief visit to one of the Osage villages before the government moved them south. The wild places were his home; there he had grown to manhood, one with the wolf and the bear. He ate. He slept. He observed from afar in peace, until the day he had seen Matt Behan and remembered.

Then the snake appeared again. He had killed Behan and followed his sons to Teardrop. The snake told Luther to hide and keep a vigil above the town, and sure enough, the other three men were there, the one who had helped to kill the father and the other two that Luther had espied through a gap in the rubble, the other two who came to take the father's pretty stones.

Snake marked them all and brought death twice again. There were others, too, who had crossed the path of the snake and had been struck down. For once the snake reappeared, it grew increasingly restless and angry.

Luther moved from his hiding place and loped

down the treacherous incline, his wolf-hide-covered feet digging into the mud. He moved effortlessly, as surefooted as any predator, down the slope, down to the world of men. He passed unseen and darkness was his friend.

The Osage Kid doctored his glass of punch with a measure of bourbon, took a sip, and found it suited him. Bannister had stolen Dancin' away and O'Brian suffered silently, he had plans for her later tonight. Journey stood close by, but he had the feeling the black woman was even less welcome than the Osage Kid. Journey shifted uncomfortably and retreated around the table to take a seat on an abandoned length of pew resting against the back wall.

A shadow fell across the Kid and he turned as Ezra brought Katrina to the table. O'Brian's gaze locked with Katrina's. She raised her eyebrows, smiled provocatively, and gave a toss of her head like a saucy, playful colt.

"What do you suggest, Mr. O'Brian?" she asked. "The sweet-potato casserole or the honey cakes?"

O'Brian looked around at the array of homemade delectables that crowded the table. He shrugged, poked a finger in the sweet-potato casserole, and came away with a morsel of food he presented to the teacher.

"Taste and decide for yourself," he answered, daring her.

Katrina moved closer and closed her lips around O'Brian's extended finger.

Ezra put himself between them, his jealousy instantly aroused.

"What the hell are you up to, O'Brian?" Ezra said, glowering, his features even more arrogant in anger. He caught Katrina's arm and pulled her away. "Go visit with Nellie Sammons," he ordered.

"All she can talk about is her new baby," Katrina sighed. "Anyway, I am not some servant for you to order about." She turned back to the table. "I think I'll take a honey cake."

Ezra cursed and stalked off through the church, back to his own circle of friends. When Ezra was safely out of earshot, Katrina smiled with satisfaction, and said, "I think I have him ready."

"For what?" asked O'Brian.

"To propose," she replied. "Your showing up was perfectly timed."

"Glad to have been of help," O'Brian added wryly.

"I'm glad you're not in jail anymore, really. And just because I'm married doesn't mean we can't be friends," Katrina said. She finished the cake and dabbed at her lips. "Are you leaving . . . soon?"

"As soon as the ground dries out," O'Brian said. "In a day or two. My shoulder can use the rest. But don't worry, Katrina, I doubt I'll be here for the wedding." He studied her with amusement, enjoying her momentary discomfort. He wondered if Katrina knew what she really wanted. The question applied to him as well.

The teacher warmed him with a provocative glance.

Heat seemed to radiate from her and brought back memories better left buried in his mind.

Sensing his reticence, Katrina frowned. The schoolmarm had no way of knowing she meant more to O'Brian than merely a way to pass a cold winter's night, a laugh or two, then a roll in the blankets.

"I think poor Ezra's suffered enough," she remarked. "Come see me before you leave." The schoolmarm patted O'Brian's arm and, circling around the dancers, made her way to Ezra's side.

"Maybe I've already left," O'Brian muttered. He studied the people in the room. Most of them were a decent hardworking sort, maybe prejudiced toward his kind but basically common folk trying to build a life for themselves and their families here in the Ozarks. The future of this territory was out there on the dance floor visiting among themselves in groups of twos or threes. In his own quieter moments he even envied their lives, envied the comfortable sameness of being with the woman you love. He loved Katrina. Oh, now he had admitted to himself. But her future was already claimed by Ezra Behan. O'Brian sighed and studied Cole Anthem. Even the Texan fit in, though he stood out, tall and lanky as he was. And the lad cut a fine if stumbling figure, leading his lady through the dance.

Cole glanced in O'Brian's direction, as if sensing his scrutiny, and a sheepish grin lit his boyish features. Then he stopped in his tracks and the humor in his eyes faded. Cole saw Price staring at him. The man was drunk, and Cole could see by the man's ex-

pression he was still resentful of the fact that he had
had to back down in the saloon.

Suddenly, Price lurched past O'Brian, his right
hand reaching down the frayed hem of his coat for
his derringer. No one noticed but Cole, Mindy Lou,
and O'Brian.

Cole dropped a hand toward his own revolver, hidden in the pocket of his borrowed coat. The hammer
snagged on the inner lining. Mindy Lou stepped in
front of Cole, but the Texan shoved her out of harm's
way and tried to free his gun.

Shotgun fished a double-barreled derringer out of
his belt and aimed drunkenly at Anthem.

The Osage Kid quickly drew abreast of Shotgun,
grabbed the derringer out of his hand, and tossed the
weapon into the nearest punch bowl.

An elderly townsman, dippering up a glassful of
punch, paused, lips parted and wide-eyed, staring at
the lethal little gun aimed at him over the edge of the
cut-crystal bowl. He scratched at the silvery whiskers
covering his chin and muttered to no one in particular,
"I've doctored my home brew with a bit of gunpow-
der in my time, but this preacher's gone and throwed
in the whole dad blamed pistol."

As Shotgun spun around and came face to face
with the Osage, O'Brian parted his coat to reveal his
gun belt. He had made no pretense of disarming himself. Before Shotgun could speak, O'Brian dragged
him over to the overcoats, grabbed a familiar one, and
swung it around the man's shoulders. It was Bannister's coat, O'Brian noted, not that he cared.

"What the hell is this for?" Shotgun protested, his speech slurred.

"So you won't catch your death of cold on your way back to the Hondo," O'Brian answered. He marched the man to the door of the church and out onto the porch, gave him a shove, and closed the door in the drunkard's wake.

"Thanks," Cole said, joining the Kid back at the table.

"If anyone shoots you, it'll be me," O'Brian growled, "for butting into my setup."

"I lost three hundred dollars this morning when the good folks of Teardrop gave you back your guns," Cole explained. He hooked his thumbs in his waistband; his cuffs rode up his wrists.

"I want to thank you too, Mr. O'Brian," Harlowe's daughter interjected. She looked O'Brian squarely in the eyes. He liked that. "I hope I can do something to repay your bravery and quick action."

"You can dance with me," O'Brian suggested.

His request had caught Mindy Lou off guard. She started to accept, then paused to consider. She had never been the subject of town gossip . . . But, she decided, there was no time to start like the present.

"Why, of course," she replied. The young woman held her hand out to the Osage Kid, who flashed a devilish grin at Cole as he led his pretty companion into the lively throng.

Complaining about the likes of bandits and half-breeds, Cole turned his attention to the leftovers of the sumptuous repast Teardrop's ladies had prepared.

The elderly man standing opposite Cole leaned forward, belched, and rubbed his red-rimmed eyes to
steady his vision, He pointed at the cut-glass bowl
with the derringer jutting ominously from its contents.
"Watch the punch, my young friend," the old-timer
warned. "It's a killer."

15

Shotgun waited for an hour in the lee of a toolshed. He stamped his feet and thrust his hands deep in his pockets against the cold. In the glare of a three-quarter moon, he saw several families leave the church; wagons and carriages rolled away down Teardrop's muddy Main Street and angled off toward the darkened homes.

He recognized Ezra Behan and Katrina and enviously imagined bedding the buxom schoolmarm. A figure like Miss Horn's made a fellow think plumb kindly of education. Shotgun pulled Bannister's coat tight around him. The saloon keeper would have a chilly ride back to the Hondo, the gunman thought, grinning. Served the bastard right for taking the likes of the Osage Kid on the payroll.

The gunman shifted his stance and cradled his shotgun, which he had taken from Bannister's carriage, in the crook of his arm. No one ordered him around, Shotgun muttered to himself. First that Texan had made him back down. Then that damn half-breed had humiliated him.

Never again!

He steadied his sawed-off .12 gauge and tried to be patient. Sooner or later, Cole Anthem would have to show himself. And when he did, there'd come a reckoning by heaven. The gunman belched, and regurgitated whiskey burned the roof of his mouth. He grimaced, trying to suppress the nausea washing over him.

"C'mon, bounty-hunter," Shotgun said. He peered around the corner of the shed, focusing on the front door as he pictured Cole and Mindy Lou emerging into the moonlight and heading straight for the Harlowe wagon and team of mares tethered at the side of the church. "Right into my sights." Shotgun chuckled.

Straw crackled behind him. A footstep, someone in the shadows. His bravery melted. The gunman whirled around, panic like a claw clutching at his throat.

Shotgun stopped dead in his tracks as the muzzle of a Navy Colt pressed his ear. The blue steel dug deep and forced his head against the side of the shed.

"Drop the shotgun," O'Brian ordered. The weapon struck direct with a dull thud. "Now your pants."

"What? Like hell," Shotgun retorted.

O'Brian cocked the revolver and continued to screw it into the side of the gunman's head. "Drop your drawers."

Shotgun cursed the half-breed but did as he was told: unfastened his belt and pulled his trousers off over his boots. He straightened, his bony limbs already trembling from the cold. O'Brian retreated a couple of steps, scooped up the man's pants and shotgun.

"What the hell is your real name?" O'Brian asked.

"Ned. Ned Price," the gunman said. His long johns were threadbare and precious little insulation.

"Well, Mr. Ned Price," O'Brian said, "you can find another gun and hide out here if you like or you can get on back to the Hondo before your balls freeze solid as bird shot."

O'Brian walked away, leaving Price to his decision. The Osage Kid grinned and hummed a tune, satisfied he had defused a dangerous situation. From now on, Price would be far more furious with the halfbreed than with Cole Anthem. And it would be a while before the bastard summoned up enough courage to try anything with the Osage Kid.

Hauling back on the reins, Ezra Behan touched his foot to the brake shaft and the carriage slowed and rolled to a stop in front of Katrina's cabin. He stepped down, tethered the gelding, and held out his arms to help Katrina climb down. As her button-top boots sank into the mud, she lifted the hem of her blue cape to avoid the dirt. Katrina winced as an icy drop of water splattered against her neck. She glared at the oaken branches swaying overhead and pulled up the cowl of her cape for protection.

Ezra's arms were still encircling her waist. While she was off balance, he pressed his advantage and

kissed her. Katrina responded just enough to let him
know she wanted more. Then, gently, she pulled free
of his grasp and started toward her cabin. An amber
glow filled the unshuttered window and cast a pool of
light upon the trampled earth. She hoped the fire in
the wood stove hadn't burned out. She checked the
iron chimney and glimpsed smoke.

Good, she thought, then the cabin would still be
warm. She started toward the door.

Ezra caught her arm and forced her to face him.
"I'll stay with you," he said.

"I think not," Katrina replied.

"Why?"

Katrina bit at her lower lip, decided it was now or
never. "I love you, Ezra Behan. But I don't love what
we have. You treat me like Gage Bannister does his
trollops." She worked loose from his grasp. "I cannot
endure it anymore." She stifled a sob, brought a kerchief out, dabbed at her eyes, and surreptitiously
looked to see if her words were having any effect.

"What do you want from me?" Ezra asked.

"To be called Katrina Behan," said the schoolmistress.

"Well, now," Ezra said, stroking his chin in
thought. "Sounds like you're sayin' we tie the knot
before we share the blanket again."

"Exactly." Katrina took his hand and placed it on
her breast. Her heart beat against his palm. "I want to
be here for you, as your wife, Ezra."

Behan considered his options. Katrina was just
about the prettiest girl in Teardrop. And would prob-

ably make a man a fine wife. At least the bed would never be cold. But he didn't like the idea of her having once consorted with that bastard, Blue Elk O'Brian, something he alone among the town's residents knew. He sighed, wondering how many nights he would have to spend alone before he found another willing lady. Maybe the blacksmith's daughter... No, Mindy Lou had rebuffed him in the past. Oh, well, there were always the girls at the Hondo.

"Sorry, Katrina," Ezra said at last. "I reckon the price is too high." He gave a sympathetic wag of his head, his finely etched features betraying a sense of regret. He moved close for a farewell embrace.

"You son of a bitch," Katrina blurted out. His answer had caught her completely off guard. Katrina's hand snapped back and she gave Ezra's face a resounding slap. The blow staggered him. Tears came to his eyes. His ear rang. She hit him! No one hit Ezra Behan. No one!

As Ezra raised a fist to swing at Katrina a wild-eyed, hair-matted figure emerged from the gloom. Katrina was shoved aside, and a gnarled, three-fingered hand caught Ezra's blow.

Ezra screamed in horror, screamed as the bones of his hand were ground together in a terrible three-fingered grip. A blade, flashing like a tongue of silver fire, ripped across Ezra's belly. Then he was lifted up and thrown against the carriage, where he crumpled like a rag doll tossed aside by an errant child.

Katrina could find no voice to scream. She headed for the cabin, reached the door, and rushed inside. She

tried to close the door behind her. But the same bestial
force that had dispatched Ezra struck the oaken door
with a rough force, sending Katrina sprawling onto
the floor.

The man stepped into the light. His features had
been seared by the fire of an explosion. His long
stringy hair was thick as a nest and streaked with
white. His nose and lips were so much gnarled tissue.
The fur hides covering his body made him seem larger
than six feet tall. A stench of sweat and rancid animal
fat filled the room. He reached out for Katrina. She
screamed then. Another sharp cry of terror filled the
room as the hairy figure slammed the door shut.

Ezra dragged himself to his knees. Blood seeped
from his belly wound. He wondered if he were dying.
He reached for the wheel rim, groaned in agony as he
tried to use his broken right hand. He pulled himself
upright with his other hand, tumbled onto the floor of
the carriage, and found the revolver he kept beneath
the seat. He fired into the air, getting off three shots
that echoed through the night. As Ezra slid down into
the mud, he espied a horseman riding toward him at
a gallop. It was Jeremiah Harlowe.

Harlowe had been heading to the church social,
hoping to catch a last dance with his daughter and
sample some of the pies before the affair ended. He
had worked hard to finish repairs on Doc Fletcher's
carriage in record time.

Katrina's scream sang out once more. It was the
same outcry Harlowe had heard down on Main Street,
but he hadn't known where to go until Ezra's gun-

shots. Her scream was higher in pitch now and completely out of control. Then it stopped suddenly. Harlowe galloped past Behan's carriage, and as he did, he looked down to see Ezra, sprawled in the mud. When the blacksmith neared the cabin, a furry giant scrambled through the door and fled into the night.

As Luther raced off up the slope, Harlowe galloped after him.

"Hold there," the blacksmith shouted. "Stand fast or I'll shoot." He dragged a Spencer carbine from its boot and levered a shell into the breach.

Luther was faster than a man had a right to be. He had lived by his wits, his instincts, and his speed—a predator whose physical strength and fleetness had been honed by the Ozarks' rugged terrain in which he had struggled to survive.

Still, despite all of Luther's ability, the horseman behind him was gaining ground, closing the gap. Run, shouted the snake in Luther's belly. Faster still. Faster! Luther drew in great lungfuls of the cold damp air. His eyes streamed tears. Why had Mother made so much noise? Luther had only wanted to hold her, to be comforted, to be not alone. He'd tried to tell her, tried to quiet her, just wanted to hold, to touch . . .

He searched the ground as he picked his way toward the trees. At last he found what he was looking for, a fist-sized stone that he scooped up on a dead run.

Luther braced himself, did an about-face as Jeremiah Harlowe bore down on him, and threw the chunk of stone with the unerring accuracy of a natural hunter. He could knock a squirrel out of a treetop anytime, any day. A full-grown man on horseback was easy. The horseman fired at the same instant.

Both men went down.

O'Brian was the first to arrive from the church. He climbed out of Bannister's surrey and hurried up the path to school. He had pocketed his Navy Colt and carried the shotgun, his finger curled around both triggers.

He knelt to check Ezra, who was unconscious now but still breathing, and then proceeded to Katrina's cabin. The door stood ajar.

"Katrina," O'Brian called out, and entered. The room showed signs of a struggle. A water pitcher and basin lay in shards on the floor. A chair and an end table were overturned. A throw rug was wadded up against the wall.

The room was littered with timber from the wood box by the iron stove as if the sticks and logs had been hurled into the room. Katrina lay by the wood box. She might have been sleeping if not for the obscene angle of her head, the garish stretch of cartilage and bone that indicated a broken neck. A few strands of her chestnut hair were singed and blackened where they had fallen against the stove. Her eyes were open, staring into the void, her lips peeled back in a horrid semblance of a scream, now silent.

O'Brian heard something brush against the wall outside, and he hurried out of the cabin, a snarl on his lips, murder in his heart. As he rounded the corner, he collided with Jeremiah Harlowe.

The blacksmith collapsed against O'Brian, who gingerly lowered Harlowe to a seat on the front porch. The older man's features were washed with blood that continued to ooze from a nasty cut on his forehead.

"I got him," Harlowe gasped. "Wounded, I think. He ran off into the trees. Cried out like some animal." Jeremiah groaned aloud and tilted his head back. "Maybe I only made things worse. A wounded animal's twice as dangerous." He reached up and caught O'Brian by the front of his coat. "But you'll have to run him down. You hear me?" Harlowe sighed, and his great strength seemed to leave him as he shrank in on himself and slipped from consciousness.

Katrina . . . O'Brian straightened and his burning eyes focused on the dark hills. Katrina . . . She hadn't been a saint and never pretended to be. Still, O'Brian had loved her; for all his bravura, he cared. Her death tore at him.

"I'll run him down," O'Brian said softly, ominously.

And the hills, the dark hills waited.

16

"Oh, tarnation and thunder," Jeremiah bellowed from his bed. "It takes more'n a pop on the head to put a Harlowe under." He fidgeted with Doc Fletcher's handiwork—the bandages circling his head.

Mindy Lou rapped his knuckles and, pulling on the patchwork quilt, tucked it under his chin. Downstairs the clock chimed one, an hour after midnight. There in the confines of his bedroom, Jeremiah Harlowe felt more like his daughter's prisoner than patient.

"I need a drink, not sleep, after what I've seen this night," he insisted.

Mindy calmly offered her father a shot glass filled with a brown liquid that Jeremiah gratefully sloshed down his gullet. He grimaced and smacked his lips in obvious distaste.

"What the devil was that?"

"Just a little something Doc Fletcher mixed up to help you sleep," his daughter replied.

"I meant whiskey, dammit," Harlowe cursed.

"Mindy Lou, you try me . . ." He tried to swing his legs out of bed, but was too weak. The slats beneath the mattress groaned as he shifted his weight and sank back down on the pillows.

Mindy Lou promptly tucked his sheets and quilt beneath the mattress again.

"I won't be treated like a child."

"Then stop acting childish," Mindy exclaimed. "Now, you stay put or I'll have Cole Anthem tie you to the bed frame." Harlowe's daughter advanced on him, hands on hips, anger flashing in her eyes. She was impossible to resist, the soul of resolution. And so much like her mother that, as Jeremiah submitted to her ministrations, moisture touched the corners of his eyes.

"Very well, I can't argue with both of ye," he sighed. "You and your ma," the blacksmith added in explanation. He patted the pillow beside him; the hand-crocheted pillowcase was the last of his wife's handiwork. She had died of pneumonia a day after snipping the last stitch. Then his rough hand grew still, his callused fingers entwined in the border lace, Jeremiah's mouth dropped open, and he began to snore.

Mindy Lou leaned forward and kissed him on his stubbly cheek. When she straightened up, she saw herself in the mirror across the room. She had changed from her party dress back into a brown checkered work shirt and faded, rust-colored nankeen trousers.

The woman in the mirror seemed older than seventeen, and worry lines were etched in her face. She had followed Cole Anthem to the schoolhouse and had seen Katrina's body in the cabin out back. Mindy had covered the dead schoolmarm's garishly twisted corpse with her own woolen shaw before she returned to her father's side.

Some others had loaded Ezra Behan onto a wagon bed and had taken him to Doc Fletcher's house. After tending Behan's wounds, Fletcher had hurried to Jeremiah's side.

The town barber, acting as a part-time undertaker, was brought to the schoolhouse by Parson Perry Ford, who promised to see to Katrina's burial. Mindy Lou remembered O'Brian's odd show of concern. He had walked alongside the barber's wagon all the way back to the church, where the dead woman was placed on a table and covered with a shroud until the barber could complete a suitable coffin.

Mindy Lou wondered if O'Brian was still with poor Katrina. And why? She dimmed the oil lamp on the night table beside the bed and silently stole from her father's room.

In the stable, O'Brian held one of the gelding's hind legs and methodically trimmed the rough edges off an iron shoe he had just hammered onto the animal's hoof. Perspiration matted the Osage's black hair to his skull as he worked, shirtless, the muscles rippling over his wiry torso.

He made no effort to work quietly and did not care who came to confront him. O'Brian was reclaiming

the gelding. He knew the animal's strengths and con-
ditioning, and he did not want to trouble himself with
an unfamiliar mount. The gelding was quick, surefooted as a cat, and calm-natured for the most part,
qualities the Osage Kid could count on.

Cole, in another stall, worked the stiff-bristled
brush down the length of the roan's back. With another dozen brisk strokes, he considered himself done.
He stepped out of the stall, rinsed his hands in a
bucket of water, and then set the bucket down for the
roan to drink its fill.

The two men cleared off one of Harlowe's work-
tables and, after dismantling their weapons, arranged
the various rags, ramrods, stocks, screws, and gun
barrels across the tabletop.

Cole worked in silence. He was loath to bother
O'Brian while the man was in such a dark mood. It
puzzled the young Texan that O'Brian had taken Katrina's death so hard. Cole wondered how far back
their relationship ran. Even worse, the Osage Kid
seemed to hold himself responsible for the schoolmarm's death.

The Texan shrugged and crossed the aisle to the
worktable, ducking under a row of bridles and leather
traces that hung from a low beam near the table.
Quickly, he reassembled his own handgun, wiped it
clean of oil, and fit a loaded cylinder onto the cylinder
post and slid the barrel into place. He repeated the
process with O'Brian's Navy Colts. O'Brian joined
him at the table and began cleaning a Sharps .50 cal-

iber that looked as if it hadn't been cleaned since the end of the war.

"I'm, uh, sorry about Katrina," Cole offered, unsure whether or not he should say anything else. He continued to work a cleaning rod down the barrel of the Winchester and waited.

O'Brian made no reply, his thoughts were full of self-recrimination. It was his fault Katrina was dead. He had played a waiting game, choosing to remain in town under the pretense of a sore shoulder when the real reason had been Katrina Horn. Sooner or later he would have stolen to her bedside. It was as inevitable as the desire that had brought them together two years past. No matter her plans for Ezra Behan, O'Brian knew he could have persuaded her. Now, that would never be. And despite his carefree pretense back in Bannister's saloon, he admitted that Katrina, for all her faults, had been special to him, more so than any other woman he had ever known. Suddenly, he felt he had to talk about it.

"About two years ago, in the dead of winter, I broke into the Mercantile and stole a few necessities—a couple of blankets, tins of food, you know. Anyway, Granbury caught wind of me. I rode hell for leather out of town. But my horse threw me. I cracked some ribs, had to crawl back to town. I holed up in the first house I came to . . . Katrina's."

O'Brian paused in his account. Wood cracked and popped among the flames in the stoves at either end of the stable. The Osage Kid retrieved his shirt from a nearby sawhorse and pulled it on. A brown bottle sat atop a barrel of nails. He grabbed it, popped the cork, and washed his gullet with a measure of Bannister's finest, pilfered from the gambler's private stock back at the Hondo. Then he returned to the table and resumed his story as he carefully adjusted the sights on the buffalo gun.

"She didn't turn me in," O'Brian said, as if that were explanation enough. "My father was dead, my mother and her people shipped off to Indian territory north of the Red River. I was alone. And Katrina Horn didn't turn me in."

He balanced the rifle in his hands and began to work several years of grit out of the breech with his pocketknife, remembering cold winter nights spent in Katrina's warm bed and, later on, nightly forays to town to see her for an hour or two. But she was a proper schoolmistress and he a half-breed fugitive, and their days together were numbered. She wanted more . . . more than he could give. A twenty-four-hour life, a proper name, a family of some station and position in the community; things that a man like Ezra Behan could provide.

It had hurt to lose her, but O'Brian hadn't been able to bring himself to blame Katrina. The schoolmarm had been his lover and his friend, and now she was dead. O'Brian blew into the breech, and a cloud of black smoke billowed up toward his face. Grit stung his eyes and shattered his reverie. He returned his attention to the task at hand.

He noticed Cole was finished with the Winchester. The Texan leaned against a stall, the carbine cradled in his arms. The young man's lanky frame cast a long shadow, and though Anthem was a few years younger than O'Brian, he seemed to be listening with his heart as well as his mind.

"You better go check on Harlowe," the Osage Kid suggested.

"You can come along. Mindy'll have some pie and coffee for us."

"No, I'll find a stall and spread my bedroll in the straw and go to sleep," O'Brian replied.

Cole glanced toward the door that led to the house. He would be leaving at sunrise, and no telling when he would see the blacksmith's daughter again.

"Well, maybe I ought to pay my respects," Cole figured aloud. He glanced at the Osage Kid as if seeking approval, then kicked at the dirt and headed for the door. "I won't be long." The stable door creaked on its hinges as the Texan eased out into the darkness and vanished from sight.

"Take your time, boy," O'Brian said to the silence. He carried his bedroll to the nearest vacant stall. Climbing to the loft, he pitched an extra layer of sweet hay over the rails until the hard ground was completely hidden beneath a couple of feet of dry grass. Then he spread his blanket on it and stretched out.

But sleep was a long way off. And the night seemed darker than the Osage Kid had ever known it to be. He closed his eyes, saw her face, felt the pain well up in him. And he told her then that he loved her. And in his mind she didn't laugh. And in his mind he held her and knew her warmth again. And it helped him through the night.

Cole paused on his way to the house and silently observed what he could see of the other houses scattered around the town. It was two in the morning, but lamplights burned in every inhabited dwelling as word of Katrina's death spread like wildfire. He imagined husbands and fathers standing guard behind closed doors. A war party of prospectors armed with knife, gun, and club crossed the bridge—a noisy cluster of trigger-happy vigilantes ready to cut down the first stranger they encountered on patrol of the town.

Cole hurried to the back door of Harlowe's house. It was dark inside, but the door was unlatched, and the Texan stepped into the kitchen, grateful to be out of the chill night. He breathed deeply of the warm air laced with the scent of cinnamon and apples and roast ham. He listened, puzzled, almost fearful that Mindy Lou had gone on to bed. He didn't hear a thing. Going to the cutting table, he felt around under it for his bedroll and wondered if someone had moved it. He left his Winchester on the tabletop.

A glow from the fireplace in the sitting room illuminated the dining room as well, and beckoned by its pulsating light, he left the kitchen, eased past the dinner table and the china cabinet to stand in the foyer near the stairway that divided the front rooms.

Cole was brought up sharply at the foot of the stairs, his hand gripping a balustrade, as he espied Mindy Lou standing in the sitting room. A patchwork quilt was spread on the floor in front of the fire in the hearth. Sheets, a blanket, and another quilt turned back made an inviting bedroll. The blacksmith's daughter shifted nervously, facing Cole. She allowed a shawl to slip from her shoulders; underneath she wore a cotton nightgown that laced from her bosom to her neck.

"I've been waiting for you," she said. The firelight lent a ruby luster to her auburn hair and outlined her figure beneath the soft folds of her gown.

As Cole moved into the room, he swallowed with effort and tried to find his voice. He almost succeeded. Then Mindy Lou untied the bow and unlaced her gown and let it slide to the floor. She stood naked, the flames warming her trim, rounded hips and muscular legs.

"God in heaven, you're beautiful," Cole managed to gasp.

Mindy Lou knelt in the blankets and held her arms out to him. Cole kicked out of his boots, slid his flannel shirt off over his head, and dropped his gun belt, trousers, and flannel long johns in one quick gesture. He stepped onto the blankets and knelt opposite the young woman.

"Too much sadness, too much death. I want to feel alive," Mindy said. "You'll be gone tomorrow. I wonder if I'll see you again."

Cole could have lied, but he was cut from better cloth. Despite his urgent desire for her, Cole's own sense of pride and self-worth forced him to speak the truth.

"I don't know," he answered.

Mindy smiled in understanding. "I care about you, Cole, and I know you care about me. But how deep it runs, who can say. Maybe no deeper than this." She leaned forward and kissed his cheek. The taut pink crowns of her small breasts brushed against his chest. "Or this." She kissed his chin. "Or this." Her lips pressed to his.

Cole's arms encircled her waist, his manhood explored the forest of auburn ringlets between her thighs. Their bodies pressed together as the kisses became more feverish, each caress more heated than the one before.

"Be with me," Mindy whispered. She arched her back as his kisses traced a path from her neck to her breasts. He nibbled and nipped and moistened each nipple with his tongue, and when she rolled onto her back, Cole was with her, then in her. Their consummation, like the flames, wild and fierce, a oneness of flesh into flesh, passion and a search for affirmation.

To feel the fiery power of love is to be alive.

They asked nothing in return, made no promises, no demands. They had only one night to know life, to burn together in desire, to know the giving and the sharing as two became one, climaxing, rushing from peak to peak, with a groan, a sigh, a gentle sob, and to sink into the wondrous warmth of each other's arms.

He remained hard in her. She locked her legs around his back and gasped out each shuddering spasm. Cole buried his face in the crook of Mindy's neck, embarrassed at the tears that threatened to spill down his cheek. It had been a long lonely trail from Texas to the war to prison and release, to the day a boy became a man and rode the bounty trail.

"Thank you," he said, softly, tasting the salt on her sweat-streaked chest, hearing her heartbeat, feeling her pulse, knowing her with all his senses.

"Thank you," she sleepily replied.

Embers crackled and popped, the firelight danced, and darkness could not prevail against it.

17

Cole and the Osage Kid rode out of Teardrop with the glassy orange eye of a newly risen sun at their backs. They rode alone, but they carried the hopes of the townsfolk with them. Abigail Ford had provided more than good wishes, she brought the two men new clothes from the Mercantile, a gift they had gratefully accepted.

O'Brian traded his trail-worn trappings for a gray flannel shirt and brown canvas Levi's and a broad-brimmed hat to shade his dark eyes. Cole replaced his Confederate-issue gray with a coarsely woven brown cotton shirt, a leather vest, and black woolen trousers. Both had heavy buckskin coats. Anthem's Colt was holstered high on his hip. O'Brian wore his revolver lower on the thigh, strapped down, the gun butt thrust slightly forward. His hideout gun rested against the small of his back, concealed beneath his coat. He sat slouched, relaxed . . . free and easy. Free. The Osage Kid was no man's prisoner; he was Blue Elk O'Brian, the last of his kind in this rugged country, a stranger in his own homeland, but he refused to be moved or shoved out of these wild and haunted hills.

Cole no longer considered O'Brian his prisoner. In fact, the Texan's thoughts were focused on only one thing: the young woman standing in the doorway of her home, her hand raised to wave, almost beckoning him back. But Cole knew he could not turn back. Not until the job he had set for himself was completed: they would find the crazed killer or he would find them.

Harlowe's daughter had whispered to Cole, in parting, a simple entreaty, "Be careful." It pleased Cole the way Mindy Lou had said it, close enough that her lips brushed his cheek in a shy kiss. O'Brian, astride the chestnut gelding, had looked away with a grin.

The two men left unannounced. And why should there be fanfare? O'Brian grimly reflected. More than likely we'll be just another two corpses for someone to find in a cave, beneath a red oak, or floating face-down and freshly butchered in a creek bed . . . Then again, maybe not. He shifted the weight of the Sharps .50 caliber cradled in his arms. Long-range death . . .

"We could hold off till the burying," Cole suggested, misreading his companion. Cole looked toward the cemetery where its markers like signposts signaled the end to earthly journeys.

"I've said my good-byes," O'Brian replied dryly. He had no wish to see Katrina's grave. As he nudged his heels into the flanks of his horse, the animal obediently broke into an easy canter, a distance-eating gait that Cole's mount quickly matched. The forested slope drew closer, the road became a series of wheel ruts, then little more than a deer trail.

Cole took one last look at the town and noticed a procession of wagons and pack mules winding their own way out of town. More prospectors and their families were leaving. They had packed up what few possessions they owned, gathered together for safety, and abandoned their camps along the Crazy Head.

The prospectors were the lifeblood of the community, a major source of income along with the farmers in the area. Cole doubted the town could survive without the prospectors. And what of the farmers? Some of the newcomers had already pulled stakes and quit. Others were talking of doing the same.

Teardrop was dying and Cole Anthem wondered if there was anything he really could do to save it. Well, not the whole town, but a part of it named Mindy Lou.

Gage Bannister hadn't slept, and looked it. He climbed down from his carriage, patted imaginary dust from his finely tailored clothes, and wiped the grit from his spectacles. His wasn't the only carriage in front of Elizabeth Behan's. The parson's carriage was tethered at a post a few yards away.

Anthem and the Osage Kid had left an hour earlier. And Bannister had quickly dispatched Shotgun Ned Price to a certain cabin back in the hills where a very important guest was quartered. One plan was in motion; the second, however, appeared to be out of control.

Elizabeth Behan's stableman had brought news that Teardrop's most important family was preparing to abandon the town. Gage Bannister did not like to be crossed. He had counted on Elizabeth's support, no matter how unwilling. Well, it shouldn't take long to put the woman in her place, Bannister decided, and he slicked back his silver hair. His pale round features took on a look of confidence and determination as he all but marched down the walk and mounted the steps to the front porch. The front door opened, to his surprise, and Elizabeth herself emerged from the house. She wore an ankle-length wool skirt, a tweed jacket, and gloves on her slender hands. Her attire was as black as her hair. Her cheeks wore a mere suggestion of rouge. She looked serious, purposeful, hardly the picture of a woman who had suffered not only the loss of a husband but the maiming of a son.

"I expected you," she said in an icy tone. "Nothing is a secret in Teardrop . . ." She paused and corrected herself, "Almost nothing."

"I was worried you'd forgotten," Bannister said. He ambled toward the nearest of the rocking chairs that Elizabeth kept on the porch.

"You're leaving for Little Rock, I know," said the owlish-looking gambler. "But when are you coming back? You know I have a keen interest in your whereabouts as we're partners." He eased into a rocking chair, inhaled deeply, a ridge of belly fat rolled over the top of the black sash circling his waist. "I'll take some of that coffee I smell." He shifted in the chair and adjusted the gun butt poking out of his waistband.

"You won't be staying long enough to enjoy it," Elizabeth replied. Her small-boned, delicate-looking appearance was an illusion, Bannister thought. She stood straight and tall and full of fight. He liked that in a woman just as long as she knew her place when it came to Gage Bannister's wishes and wants.

"Ezra will need proper care. But he will recover from his wounds, and when he does, I intend to take my family to Natchez. We will make our lives there." Elizabeth folded her arms across her chest, steadied herself, and waited for his threat.

"It takes money to start over. And a good reputation don't hurt," Gage purred. "Neither of which you'll have when folks learn how Matt Behan came by his fortune."

The front door opened and Reverend Perry Ford stepped out from the sitting room. His black frock coat was unbuttoned and his shirt wrinkled and stained with Ezra Behan's blood. Toast crumbs dotted his black beard, his eyes were bloodshot and pouchy from lack of sleep.

Bannister halted in midsentence, loath to pursue a public confrontation. The parson nodded to Elizabeth and propped his hip on the porch railing. He held a cup of steaming coffee to his lips and finished the last of the black brew the maid had poured for him.

"Doc Fletcher did a good job," Parson Ford said. "Ezra's ready to travel." He reached up to touch the brim of his round, broad-rimmed hat and realized he had left it inside. His cheeks reddened; he looked foolish and knew it. "Uh . . . Good morning, Mr. Bannister, surprised to see you so early. A man in your profession usually sleeps late."

"Sometimes, Parson. But men in my profession are by nature—how shall I say, opportunistic. We make hay while the sun shines." Bannister grinned. "Now if you'll excuse us, me and the lady have business."

"I have nothing to hide from the reverend," Elizabeth said. She shivered as a cool breeze stirred the dust where the horses were tethered and rustled the branches of the sweet gum trees about the house. "He knows everything. About my husband's crime and your pitiful attempt at coercing me into some sort of dreadful alliance. Your misfortunes are of no concern to me."

Bannister's eyes momentarily widened in alarm. He stopped rocking in the chair. "Oh?" His gaze fixed on the parson.

"Yes," Ford replied. "And I've offered Mrs. Behan the benefit of my advice." The reverend stared at his empty cup, unable to meet the gambler's stare.

"Perry reminded me that you have much more to lose than I, should the authorities ever learn of your complicity with Matt Behan," Elizabeth said. "But don't worry. As long as you keep away from me, you'll have nothing to fear. My sons and I are leaving, today, Mr. Bannister, and there is nothing you can do or say that will stop me."

Elizabeth advanced on the gambler as he sat still, thoughtful, his expression grim.

"I intend to arrange for the sale of all my holdings and try to set right what I can during my stay in Little Rock. Then leave for Natchez. And you, sir, will have to survive without my help."

Bannister slowly rose from the chair and faced Elizabeth. She would not be moved, nor did she retreat from his angry glare. He moved around her, walked toward the steps, and paused alongside Ford.

"You played a poor hand, taking a chair in this game, preacher," Bannister said in a malevolent tone.

"God has taken a chair, why not I?" Ford replied. "This town has prospered on the blood of innocents, thanks to you and Matt and the rest. Now the justice of Jehovah, the fire of the Lord that suited the Philistines, has caught this town, it will burn our community clean of guilt." The reverend found his courage then and straightened, drew himself up to confront the gambler.

"Elizabeth hopes to atone for the sins of her husband. But what of you, Gage Bannister, what of you?" Ford shook his head and raised his eyes toward heaven. "You come to threaten and intimidate, better that you fall to your knees and beg the Lord for forgiveness. Entreat your Creator, or ye shall follow the path of Matt Behan and Granbury and the poor girl we bury today. You're next, Gage Bannister. You're—"

"No!" Elizabeth shouted, too late.

The gambler's fist shot up and caught the parson

beneath the chin. The force of the blow lifted the preacher off his feet and flung him over the railing. He landed on his shoulder and rolled onto his back in the snow-covered flower bed fronting the house.

Bannister cursed, licked his bruised knuckles, and turned to face Elizabeth again. She seemed in shock, startled by his sudden savage attack on a man of God. Bannister took a step toward the woman; behind the thick lenses of his wire-rim spectacles his eyes had turned hard and brutal. Elizabeth began to retreat, backing along the porch. Bannister grinned. The woman was frightened now. He liked that. Then the ominous click of a gun being cocked stifled his enjoyment. He turned and saw Jordan Behan standing at the corner of the house. Two field hands flanked him. Only Jordan was armed. He aimed a big .45-caliber Colt Dragoon at the gambler.

Below the porch, Parson Ford clambered to his feet, rubbing his swollen jaw as blood seeped from his split lip. He leaned against the railing for support.

"I don't hold with listening to pulpit-thumpers," Jordan said. "And I don't cotton to no church social and such silliness when there ain't nothing to feel good for," Behan continued. "But lifting a hand against a man of God is wrong in any book."

"Put the gun away, Behan. You haven't the stomach for a killing. You won't shoot me just for giving this meddling bastard what he deserves," Bannister said, his hand creeping toward his belly gun.

"Maybe not," Jordan conceded, "but I'll not have you bother my ma. For that I'll shoot you dead." The field hands began putting some distance between themselves and Elizabeth's eldest son. Jordan took no notice of them. The big man waited, his revolver steady in his hand. The breeze seemed to tug at his thinning hair, and his expression was calm but implacable.

Bannister studied Jordan a moment more, then stretched out his arms, palms open, and smiled.

"Every dog ought to have his day," he said matter-of-factly. Swinging around, he bowed slightly to Elizabeth, then hurried down from the porch. He completely ignored the parson, climbed aboard his carriage, and with a flick of the reins pulled away from the house of Behan.

Jordan holstered his gun. Motioning for the field hands to take the rocking chairs off the porch, he instructed them to store the chairs in the stable.

"My thanks for ending a most unpleasant situation, young man," Reverend Ford said, nursing his jaw.

"Who said it was ended?" Elizabeth remarked. "I've done you a terrible disservice," she continued. The widow wished she had never gotten Ford involved.

"Never fear," the reverend said. His lip was swollen and discolored, but at least the bleeding had stopped. He reached in his coat pocket and brought out a worn leather-bound Bible, its pages curled and torn at the edges, the spine wrinkled from many years of study. "The word of the Lord shall be my sword and shield." He patted the Bible and returned it good-naturedly to his frock coat. He darted up the steps and into the house only to reappear with his hat and duster in hand. Ford wished her well again and departed.

Elizabeth watched the kindly figure climb into his trap and head toward town. A man of simple, uncomplicated faith. She hoped his Bible would work better against a bullet than it had against Bannister's fist.

Shotgun Ned Price was waiting outside the carriage shed at the rear of the Hondo. His slim solid figure detached itself from the shadows and strode out into the sunlight past the three horses rigged with McClellan saddles.

Bannister guided his carriage to a halt directly in front of the shed where a young black boy waited to lead the mare to water. As Bannister climbed down, Price hurried to meet him.

"We just arrived. The others are inside. I was coming to get you." Price cradled his .12 gauge in the crook of his arm and jerked his thumb toward the back door of the Hondo. "I told 'em to stay in your office."

"Good," Bannister replied. His meeting with Elizabeth Behan had left him in a foul mood, and it was getting worse with every passing minute. "Glad to see you didn't lose your pants along the way."

Price scowled and stared at the ground. He had taken quite a ribbing from Bannister's crowd after the incident with the Osage Kid. Last night Price had gone slinking into the Hondo, shivering in his mud-caked woolen underwear. But he had endured every catcall, every insult, and counted them all. That count was how many times Price was planning to shoot the Osage Kid. The way Price figured it, he wouldn't leave enough of O'Brian left to scoop up in an envelope. Price didn't reply to Bannister. He shrugged, shoved a scarred hand in his coat pocket for warmth, and stepped aside as the gambler headed for his office.

The morning sun slowly leached the chillness from the air, and though the breeze remained cool, patches of snow were transformed to muddy ground and miniature ponds, glassy in the sunlight. The earth sucked at Bannister's boots as he crossed the yard to his office. He scraped the soles clean on the back steps and hurried inside.

"About time. I don't like to be kept waiting," Major Andrew Kedd declared in an imperious tone of voice. He was seated on the edge of Bannister's desk, one leg dangling above the floor. His round brimmed military hat, its black plume sleek and shiny, rested in the middle of the desktop. Private Pepper Fisk, his potbelly thrust forward like a bay window, leaned against the far wall near the door to the interior of the saloon. His lips were thick and dry and his expression betrayed a driving desperation for a bottle of anything.

J. D. Canton stood near a bookshelf staring with incomprehension at the titles, sounding the words to himself. He lowered his perplexed gaze and found a *Police Gazette* and his yellow-toothed grin betrayed his delight. The hell with fancy books, here was reading worthy of a man.

"My apologies, Major Kedd," Bannister said in a soothing tone, and he tossed his hat onto a row of pegs jutting from the wall. He smoothed his hair and smiled.

"There's been nothing but troubles of late," the gambler continued. "Not that it's any excuse. I've always prided myself on my punctuality." He shoved a tray and decanter of brandy across the desk to the major, who settled into a cushioned chair opposite Bannister.

"See here, I've played your little game long enough. As you instructed, we hid in your hunting cabin back in the hills. I endured such uncomfortable nonsense because you said you could deliver the Osage Kid into my hands." Kedd made a dramatic show of searching the room. He craned his head to right and left and even went so far as to search under the desk. "I don't see him, Bannister. If this has been some kind of trick . . ." The major sat erect, eyes narrowed to slits, head raised so that his silvery goatee pointed accusingly at the man behind the desk.

"You wound me, sir," Bannister said, raising a pudgy hand, palm outward to indicate his innocence. "I can take you to the Osage Kid and Cole Anthem on the instant. But first, a favor, please. There is something I should like to discuss in private." Bannister nodded to Shotgun Ned Price, who stood at attention, his sun-darkened features devoid of emotion. Price walked across the room, opened the door to the saloon hall, and waited for Canton and Fisk to follow him.

Journey noticed the door was ajar and rose from a table in a flurry of feathers and French silks, leaving a trio of farmers who had been hoping to compromise what there was left of her virtue.

She stood in the doorway and the heavy scent of French perfume flowed into Bannister's office. She cocked her hip, grinned, and winked at Canton, who stared in utter amazement, his mouth hanging loose as if his jaw were broken. Journey's dark coffee-colored breasts were tantalizingly visible beneath swirls of vanilla silk that formed the bodice of her creamy white dress.

"You need somethin' from me, Mr. Bannister?" the prostitute asked.

"Yes," the gambler replied. "If the major will permit, take these two fine troopers here, the corporal and private, and show them just how high the stairway is." Bannister chuckled and sipped from a crystal goblet of brandy. "Some men say it reaches all the way to heaven."

The *Gazette* slid from Canton's fingers. Fisk propped himself against the wall and glanced at the major, who pondered the matter for what seemed to both Regulators to be an eternity. Finally Kedd nodded, muttering a complaint that all of this was highly irregular. J. D. Canton and Pepper Fisk practically trampled each other in their haste to be first through the door as Journey, masking her distaste, obediently showed them the way.

Shotgun followed the two men out of the office and, nodding to Bannister, closed the door behind him.

Major Kedd accepted a glass of brandy, chanced a

sip, and found its fruity aftertaste to his liking. He
adjusted his cartridge belt and settled into the velvet
cushioned chair to listen. By nature an impatient man,
Kedd spoke up to challenge the gambler.

"All right sir, we are alone. Let me warn you, I am
a gentleman and it will take more than the presence
of some harlot to arouse my interest. Now what do
you want to talk about?"

"Diamonds," Bannister softly began in a silken
voice, his eyes glittering behind his spectacles. "And
how you and I can be rich men. Very rich men."

Major Andrew Kedd was interested.

18

Luther was tired and his side ached terribly, making every step agony. He wanted to lie down and rest in the sun, maybe even fall asleep here on this bluff, here where the trees parted and the sun had warmed the eroded surface of limestone, yes, a good place to stretch and maybe let the pain seep from his blood-caked side into the earth. But the snake in his belly said, Climb. And Luther did as he was told.

Why had she screamed? Mother . . . He tried to quiet her. Be quiet. They'll hear. They'll come and kill me. But the more she struggled, the tighter he had to hold her. Then she went limp in his arms as her neck cracked and the blood came to her mouth. So he let her drop. No, it was their doing, not his, not his. Mother . . .

Luther pulled himself up the last few yards of the trail and gasped as his weary legs carried him along the sandstone bluff.

The air was clean and fragrant with the scent of

distant pines, and the deer trail was easy to follow as
it wound among the oaks and skirted the edge of the
bluff. Not far to go now, he would reach the cave
soon. There he could rest and nurse his wounds. Luther followed the bluff for another quarter-mile before
turning uphill once again. The trail swung back
through the trees and up a second cliff set back from
the first. It was delicate going, a path barely wide
enough for a man or a white-tailed buck and steep
enough to put a strain on the wounded man. Pain
dogged his every step, his side felt on fire, and tears
stung his eyes.

Luther wanted more than anything to lie down, to
just simply stop, but the snake refused to allow it. So
Luther King, deranged and sorely wounded, continued
climbing, driven ever onward to seek the shelter of
his cave—the only home he knew. A poor young man
hounded by an inner voice that he long ago had
ceased to recognize as his own.

Luther.

Who spoke his name? Only the keening wind here
on the crest of the broken-backed ridge. He looked
down the trail, his legs trembling and his chest heav-
ing from the climb. He was a good hunter, the best
in these hills now that the Osage people of the hills
were gone. His heart grew heavy. He missed their
kindness.

Men will come, the snake in his belly warned, and
they will try to hurt you like the soldiers, like the
people of the town. As Luther pulled the bone-
handled knife from his belt and held it on high to

catch the sunlight on the jagged-edged blade, he loosed a guttural, throat-wrenching cry that lost itself in echo upon echo. Luther had pretty stones to put in their mouths, he was strong and his knife was strong. He would hide in his lair and wait. Let them come. These men wanted the pretty stones. He would give them to them. Let them *eat* the stones like the others he had killed. He would shove the pretty stones in their mouths.

Luther sheathed the knife and trotted toward the forested hills sweeping up to the north, the product of some vast upheaval aeons ago. His side ached terribly, but he no longer dwelled on the pain—only his mission.

19

Three days' ride away from Teardrop, Cole and the Osage Kid pitched camp in a grove of flowering redbud trees. About thirty yards along, there was a spring-fed pond whose sandy shore was marked with the tracks of panther, white-tailed deer, black bear, fox, and boar. At sunset, the sky turned a burnt umber above the western bluffs while the ridges assumed a veneer of dark emerald that deepened downslope into obsidian.

As day died, Cole stretched his hands out to the campfire, grateful for the warmth and the cheer the small blaze instilled in him. His brief stay in Teardrop had changed him. Jeremiah Harlowe's hospitality made him hungry for home. His thoughts trod a precarious path between Luminaria, the Anthem ranch set deep in the harsh desert mountains of West Texas, where his family, who thought that he had died in the war, waited; and Mindy Lou, back in Teardrop, who knew he was very much alive indeed.

Several thick slices of bacon sizzled in a cast-iron skillet held above the flames. The biscuits and beans were already prepared. Cole watched with growing impatience as O'Brian flipped the crisping slices one last time and then, reading the younger man's mood, nodded in accord and muttered, "Hell, yes, the bacon's done enough for me too."

He forked about half of the contents of the skillet onto Cole's plate as Cole dished up an equal share of beans and biscuits. Both men fell to eating, hunger overruling any need for conversation. It wasn't until O'Brian poured himself a cup of black coffee and stretched out, and Cole sopped up the last bit of gravy from his plate, that the Texan remarked on the Indian's prowess as a tracker.

"My pa's one of the best trailsmen in West Texas and he taught me to read sign. And I figure I learned mighty good. But I swear I can't see what you're latching on to. I was with you the first day, but since then I've been lost as a worm in a blizzard." Cole filled a cup from the coffeepot and stretched out on his bedroll. The branches of the redbuds stirred, their rose- and lavender-bedecked limbs signaling the passage of a dusk-born breeze, and the earth released what warmth it had stolen from the sun. In the lengthening shadows, the wild things stirred. Nighthawks streaked across the deepening hues of heaven, swift and sure against a tableau of clouds. A barred owl dropped from its perch in the topmost branches of a neighboring oak and swooped off through the woods emitting a high-pitched shriek that rose the hairs on the back of Cole's neck.

O'Brian appeared to take no notice of the night-sounds. He sipped his coffee, sighed, and kicked a glowing ember that had popped from the fire back into the blaze.

"There is no sign," he matter-of-factly replied. "I'm not following any tracks, just a hunch." Toying with the tribal beads and shellwork he wore around his neck, he pondered how much to tell his youthful companion.

"A hunch?" Cole exclaimed. "You mean we left this killer's trail so you could play a hunch?" He bolted upright and sloshed coffee on his knee, then tossed the remainder of the brew aside. "Damn and all this time I thought we were closing in on the bastard."

"We are," the Osage Kid replied, the flames mirrored in eyes as black as the night-shrouded hills.

Cole thought about that. Finally, with a frown, he offered, "You knew all along how to find Granbury's and Katrina's killer and . . . Dammit, man, why didn't you say something?"

"I wasn't certain until I talked to Harlowe the night Katrina was killed."

"Well, who or what kind of devil are we up against?"

"I don't know who he is," O'Brian began. "But my people called him Shadowwalker. Years ago, before the war, he stumbled into our village, cold and near starved, but wild-eyed, as if the Great One had touched him. He did not speak and he moved like a creature of the forest. His face looked as if he had been burned by lightning." O'Brian's voice softened as he remembered. Touching the shell necklace his mother had given him before he rode away to join Stand Watie and the other red men who had fought for the Confederacy in hopes of winning back their tribal lands, he continued. "My mother and the other women of our village gave him food and clothing. He never stayed for more than a few hours, and came and went like the shadows of the forest. The Osage were his friends—or if not friends, at least we shared these hills in peace. Once a group of us young men tracked him from our village on the Buffalo to his cave back in the mountains."

"And that's where we are bound?"

O'Brian nodded. "He never raised a hand against us. I don't understand what has happened with him. But then a lot of things have changed. The village of my mother is gone and Shadowwalker has become like a mad wolf, a killer. And I must stop him."

Cole started to reply, but O'Brian gestured for the Texan to be quiet. Suddenly, the Kid bolted upright and reached for the Sharps as he stared toward the night-blackened forest to his right.

Cole snatched up the Yellowboy and rolled out of the firelight a few seconds after O'Brian. He scrambled up alongside the Osage, who crouched motionless behind a fallen tree. They waited, allowing their eyes to adjust to the darkness. Cole eased the hammer back on his carbine. O'Brian touched his arm in a gesture of restraint, then motioned Cole to follow a course parallel with him to the right. Cole nodded, assuming that O'Brian had heard or seen something move in the night.

The Texan didn't relish being far from O'Brian. One man wasn't enough to handle the Shadowwalker. Hell, two men, fully armed, hadn't been enough, Cole reminded himself, thinking of the sheriff's men he had helped to bury. Still, he kept his misgivings to himself, and when the Osage climbed over the log, Cole moved away to the right.

Fireflies circled and brushed against Anthem's coat. His boots crushed leaves, twigs popped underfoot no matter how carefully he placed his steps. Five yards, ten, through woods as black as a witch's heart. Fifteen, twenty, and Cole's grip tightened on the carbine. He felt as if he'd been walking for a lifetime now. Where the hell was O'Brian? Time to stop, join up together. What was that? Damn, something moving . . . closer . . . closer . . . Now it stopped. Cole's finger tightened on the Winchester's trigger. He chose his steps wisely, trying to feel through the soles of his boots the proper place to put his weight. He wanted his back against a tree before facing whatever had stirred in the thicket ahead.

He reached an oak, a stately old growth whose trunk rose above the neighboring redbuds to spread a latticework of branches against the sky. Cole braced himself against the oak as he brought the gun to bear and waited. And despite the brisk chill of the night, he began to sweat.

Suddenly, the thicket rattled, twigs cracked, and a ghostly shape leapt from cover to dart across the moonlit clearing. Cole snapped the carbine up and only by the merest fraction of a second avoided embarrassing himself as a white-tailed doe scampered into view. It headed straight for the Texan, caught sight of him at the last moment, and leapt away at almost a ninety-degree angle. Like a will-o'-the-wisp the animal vanished in the darkness but the sound of its passage cut through the stillness and continued for several moments. Up ahead, the Osage Kid stepped from the thicket and hurried toward Cole.

He could tell the Osage was angry. The Texan suspected O'Brian was also just as relieved as he was, and he wasn't about to put up with any of the Kid's wiseass remarks.

"There went supper," O'Brian said in an exasperated tone. "What were you waiting for?"

"I needed it to come just a little closer."

"Closer. And you claim to be a crack shot."

"Gunshots carry," Cole replied, as if lecturing a novice. "I aimed to use my teeth and bite the damn thing to death."

"Humm," O'Brian muttered, gravely accepting everything the younger man said. "They breed *men* in Texas." The merest hint of a smile tugged at the corners of his mouth. Then he turned serious again, glanced around at the shadows, and shrugged. Seventy feet away, their small campfire cast a cheery and inviting glow.

"C'mon," O'Brian said. "There's nothing else about."

Cole nodded in assent and they headed back to the clearing. The roan heard them coming, neighed, pawed at the earth, and pulled at the stake. But Cole had securely ground-tethered the roan and the animal could retreat no farther than the length of the rope looped around its neck.

He walked up to the horse, caught the tethering rope, and spoke low and soothingly. With his hand, he stroked the roan's soft neck.

"Easy, now. Only thing out yonder is the dark," Cole said in his calming tone. With his back to the forest, he didn't notice Shotgun Price disassociate himself from the silhouette of a ninebark bush and vanish, catlike, past the huge oak Cole had been braced against earlier.

"Nothing to be afraid of," Anthem continued as Bannister's hired gun crept away. "Nothing at all."

Major Andrew Kedd listened with interest as Price reported to Gage Bannister on the whereabouts of O'Brian and Anthem. The major's conscience was bothering him. However, he intended to bring it under control before it did any damage. After all, he certainly planned to bring in the Osage Kid. What was the harm in a slight delay? Kedd had always considered himself a man of honor, a gentleman, a man above temptation.

Three days ago, in Bannister's office, Andrew Kedd had learned the selling price of such a thing as honor. Bannister had made his case succinctly and well. A killer was loose with diamonds to spare . . . as the gambler so delicately put it. Whoever tracked the killer to his hideout might well find a fortune in raw gems, possibly even the source of the precious stones. Who better to find the killer than the half-breed outlaw and the bounty-hunter from Texas? Let them do the work, then Bannister and Kedd could step in and reap the benefits. Of course, Canton and Fisk didn't need to know their major's arrangement with Bannister. Since Shotgun Price worked for a share of the profits, he could be trusted not to reveal to anyone the possibility of a diamond find.

Kedd couldn't see how the plan could miss. Either way, he wound up with O'Brian. He searched in his coat pocket for his silver watch and held it out in the moonlight. Bannister had suggested a cold camp for the duration of their pursuit. It wouldn't do to alert the Osage Kid to their presence.

Kedd opened the watch and studied the tintype of his wife, her features faint in the moonlight. Of course Kedd knew every line, every sweep of her long brown tresses, the bright and truthful way she had of looking into a man, the way she made a man feel. A proper Philadelphia-bred lady, she was, waiting for him to finish his tour of duty in the Reconstruction state. She was also hoping his battlefield commission would be restored, as she longed for the prestige that went with being a general's wife. Maybe he would bring her a sack full of diamonds instead.

Kedd closed the watch, returned it to his pocket, and settling down in his blankets, tried to sleep.

Price finished his report. "I thought they had me for sure. The doe was a lucky break." He poured another measure of Bannister's whiskey for himself and gulped it down.

"Good. You didn't hear anything else."

"Only that the breed seems to have someplace in mind, 'cause he ain't reading any sign." Price headed for his own bedroll and stretched out. He fished a can of cold beans from his saddlebag, worked the tin open with the blade of his knife, and began to eat, using the knife for a fork.

"Very well," Bannister said beneath his breath. He rose from the outcropping of granite that had been his bench and sauntered out of the clearing toward the horses. The gambler's tailored attire had taken a beating. His trousers were blotched with mud and he had already ripped the left shoulder of his fur-lined coat on a bramble bush. He had ceased to care. Pretty soon he would be able to afford a hundred coats if he played his cards right. And no more squandering his money. He would invest it wisely, like Matt Behan had done, and not just run whores and gambling halls. He would buy land and livestock. Too bad for Matt, for Granbury, for McKeil . . .

"I'm left," Banister muttered as he moved among the horses. He made sure the tether rope was securely tied to the two oaks Canton had chosen. The trees were twenty-five feet apart, which left ample room for all five horses to be tied to the string.

"I'm left," Gage Bannister said again, and the realization made him feel terribly alone. Who was it up there? John King was dead, Gage and Matt had made certain with a half-dozen well-placed slugs. Was it the boy? He would be in his twenties now. But Gage himself had seen the explosion that brought the mountain down in an avalanche of boulders and rubble and sealed the entrance. And yet, could the boy have lived, escaped by some other route? Many a cave had more than one entrance. Yes, Gage Bannister thought, reaching the same conclusion as he had days ago.

The deaths of Katrina Horn and the others may have been accidents or committed on purpose to keep the gambler from suspecting the killer's real motives. But Bannister's three accomplices were dead, each with a diamond left in his mouth, like a signature. These were indisputable facts. Gage Bannister was next on the killer's list.

But the gambler was not a man to wait like a sheep bound for slaughter. He would meet his attacker head-on. And this time he would learn the secret of John King's diamond find.

A twig cracked to his rear. Bannister whirled and drew his revolver with a speed that belied his rotund physique. The gun in his hand centered on J. D. Canton, who drew up sharply, gasped, and held up his hands. He had never seen a man of Bannister's size move so fast. The big bulky soldier steeled himself for a killing shot. "You want to die, Corporal?" the gambler hissed.

"No, sir. We just went to take a leak back in the cedar break."

"Make more noise, then," Bannister growled. "Or

you'll never see **Little Rock**." Returning his revolver
to the sash he wore around his waist, he shoved past
the Regulators and stalked angrily into the clearing
toward his bedroll.

"What the hell was that about, J. D.?" Pepper Fisk
said over his shoulder as he urinated against the trunk
of a stately oak.

"The gambler's a might jumpy," Canton replied,
wiping a forearm over his scarred face. Here, out of
sight of the major, he uncorked his canteen and took
a long drink. Rye whiskey lit a fire in his throat and
filled his belly with embers to keep him warm
throughout the night.

"Save some for me, dammit," Fisk said, his breath
clouding the cold night air. The smaller man buttoned
his fly and hurried to the corporal's side. Canton
passed him the canteen. Fisk sloshed it and frowned,
realizing how little was left.

A barred owl screeched, dived through the darkness, and fixed its talons in some kind of prey that
loosed a pitiful shriek as its back was broken. Fisk
tilted the canteen to his lips.

"There you go." Canton chuckled. "Finish it up and
you'll be a brave tin soldier again." He stared toward
the cold camp where Bannister, Kedd, and Price were
already asleep or pretended to be. Then he brought
his grizzled countenance close to Fisk. "Something
ain't right, Pepper," he whispered. "I can't put my
finger on it, but hear me. You watch my back and I'll
guard yours."

Fisk paused, swallowed, and exhaled slowly, his

eyes widening. "Uh, sure, J. D. You can count on me."

"We'll be counting on each other, all right, before this trek is done," Canton warned. He didn't know why he was worried, but he sure as hell aimed to find out.

20

O'Brian and Anthem led their horses down a dry creek bed bordered on either side by thick stands of oak and hickory and a sprinkling of dogwoods. Iron-shod hooves rang out on the dolomite surface of the creek bed as the two men followed the whitish path of stone that seemed to lead deeper into a wild and remote collection of broken hills.

Around noon it began to rain, a fine misty shower that offered no threat of flash flood as it fell from a flat gray sky. The two men donned their slickers and proceeded along in discomfort, cursing the diminished visibility. Shadowwalker wouldn't see them, but they wouldn't see him either.

Cole tilted his head and studied the creek bed, espied a couple of notched triangular stones he took for arrowheads. They were made of chert and worn smooth by rapidly running water whenever the creek flooded. A lizard scurried out from the gravel underfoot and darted toward the wooded bank. The rain shower ceased as quickly as it had begun for the second time that morning.

O'Brian lifted his hand and waved the Texan forward to join him climbing up the creek bank. Anthem drew abreast of the Osage in the shade of a hickory tree and looked down the undulating creek bed in the direction he indicated. A quarter of a mile away, Buffalo Falls spilled from a bluff overhead, fell more than thirty feet to an overhanging ledge of limestone where the age-old action of the waterfall had worn a hole about six feet in diameter through the ledge itself, and spilled over and through the layered rock in a double veil of plunging spray. Beyond the waterfall a patch of darkness indicated a cave, and Cole had the distinct impression this was their destination. The creek bed widened near the cave.

The spring itself flowed out from a pool at the mouth of the cave and down between the rocky banks for about a hundred yards before seeping into the ground. Cole imagined the torrent of underground water pulsing beneath the earth, a subterranean cave carved by the same buried stream.

O'Brian clambered back down the bank to the horses and draped his slicker over the saddle. Cole also freed himself from the cumbersome raincoat. The subtle, distant sound of thunder signaled a storm rampaging across another valley south of the bluffs.

Cole glanced at the overcast sky and watched a thunderhead slowly develop to the southwest. He hoped they would be under shelter soon because the storm appeared to be moving northeast, right toward the creek bed. He looked at O'Brian, who stood with his arms folded on the saddle, one hand propped on the Sharps riding in its saddle scabbard.

"You think he's in the cave?" Cole asked.

"Maybe," O'Brian replied. "I'd planned on holing up among the rocks outside the falls and bringing him down the minute he showed himself . . ." The Osage Kid turned his attention to the creek bed winding on ahead. It had seemed like a good idea back in Teardrop.

"And now?" Cole asked, pressing the issue. He nudged his rain-spattered hat high on his forehead and waited for the Kid's reply. Anthem tensed as O'Brian straightened up and swung into the saddle.

"Suppose we just ride up to the falls and take a look in that cave," the Osage Kid suggested.

"It'd be a daresome thing," Cole answered. "And then what?"

"If Shadowwalker's in there, let him make the play," O'Brian said. "If possible, we'll bring him back to Teardrop and have Mr. Harlowe take a look at him."

"I didn't think you had the stomach to bushwhack him," Cole said, relaxing. He eased his grip on his holstered revolver. The lanky young man remounted. He looked aside at the Kid. "I don't cut my sights that way either."

"A good thing to know." O'Brian grinned. "In case you ever start tracking me again." The smaller man chuckled, his dark eyes flashed a merry light. He checked his revolvers. He patted the Arkansas toothpick, fourteen inches of razor-sharp steel scabbarded on his left hip, and pulled the Sharps buffalo gun from the saddle boot. Cole slid the Yellowboy Winchester into his hands. The weapon was fully loaded, a .44 rimfire cartridge riding in the chamber.

"What if he's got a gun?" Cole suddenly considered. They would be riding up in full view.

"One of us ought to live long enough to cut him down," O'Brian said, smiling, as if his words were a soothing tonic.

"I feel a lot better," Cole grumbled.

O'Brian's gelding started forward but didn't hold the lead for long. Anthem's roan quickly matched the chestnut's gait. As the two men rode together, down the center of the creek bed, the roaring cascade of Buffalo Falls grew louder, ominously louder, luring them through the haunted hills.

Forty minutes later they both dismounted and left their horses in midstream, a dozen yards from the falls. The icy water came to just above the ankle, but its bracingly cold temperature seeped through boot leather and chilled flesh and bone. O'Brian angled across the stream toward the drier west side of the cave hidden behind a shimmering curtain of cold mist. Cole stared up at the layered limestone battlement from which the water sprang forth in its wild cascade to plunge through the hole in the stone ledge in an unceasing, battering force.

Cole's attention returned to O'Brian, who was standing in the water and waving for the Texan to join him. The tension returned, a tightness in his gut as he stepped forward into the unknown. Anthem cocked the Yellowboy and trotted along the bank until he closed the gap between him and the Osage Kid.

O'Brian leaned the Sharps against the outside wall of the cave, balancing the weapon on the lichen-dappled rocks where a patch of columbine sprouted from what seemed a sheer stone. He drew his Navy Colt and angled past the waterfall and into the patch of darkness beyond. Cole clenched his teeth, his features a mask of determination as he entered the cave.

It wasn't as dark as he had expected. The gray glare of the overcast day shone through the falls and offered bleak but adequate illumination. The chamber ran about twenty-five feet back into the cliff. Its floor of sculpted smooth dolomite rose up nearly a foot from the plunging waterfall, which kept the cave from being flooded.

The ceiling was seamed and fissured, and in places, water that had worked its way down from the bluff above seeped through the cracks in the stone. Moss gave a greenish tint where it covered the ceiling near the mouth of the cave.

Cole swung his rifle from left to right as if he were expecting a veritable army of demons to leap out at him. O'Brian was no less tense. The cave appeared empty, at least up front, where the daylight cast the entrance in somber relief. O'Brian probed farther, choosing his steps wisely, his revolver trained on the shadowy recesses of the chamber.

Suddenly he paused. O'Brian glanced at Cole, who nodded in affirmation. The Texan heard it too.

Breathing. They froze in their tracks and listened to fix the source of the sound. He leveled his gun at a patch of shadow that began to remove itself from the rear of the chamber and shuffle forward, feet dragging.

Luther stumbled into the dim gray daylight, his ruined features made even more ominous and threatening by the mottled glare. His clothing of crudely stitched buckskin was damp with blood from the wound in his side. He took another step forward and raised the long blade of a jagged-edged knife that he gripped in his strong right hand. Hair hung wild as a briar patch down his shoulders, a tangled beard covered his jaw, streaks of white skin showed where the whiskers failed to cover scarred flesh.

"Hold it right there," Cole said. And Luther's round, wide eyes shifted and bored into the Texan. He turned and took another step, this time toward Cole, who raised his Winchester and sighted down the barrel of the weapon.

A cry rose from deep in Luther's chest, grew higher in pitch until it became a piercing shriek that turned the young Texan's blood cold and rippled his flesh with goose pimples. Anthem tightened on the trigger.

"Be quiet," O'Brian said, but he spoke the words in Osage and, holstering his gun, strode forward, placing himself between Anthem and the man called Shadowwalker.

"You're blocking me," Cole exclaimed. The Osage ignored his warning. He continued moving toward the man with the knife. A look of surprise showed in Lu-

ther's desperate, demented stare. He recognized the
Osage dialect.

"We will not hurt you," O'Brian spoke, again in
the tongue of his mother's people.

Luther faced him, still threatening with the knife.
But his eyes lowered, then brightened with recognition. He reached out and touched the rawhide string
of shells and beadwork O'Brian wore about his neck.
As Luther recognized the handiwork, his tortured features softened, the knife lowered.

"Friend," he said. And collapsed in O'Brian's arms.

It rained that afternoon and the storm continued, un-
abated, into the evening. The horses had been brought
inside the cave and tethered against the east wall.
Cole found enough dry kindling in the cave to start a
fire and make coffee. In the dim light, O'Brian dug a
lead slug out of the unconscious man's side and
drenched the ruptured flesh with whiskey, then he
cauterized the wound by heating a knife blade in the
flames of the campfire and touching the reddish steel
to the man's bloody side.

The irony of the situation wasn't lost on Cole. They
had come to kill this man and now were trying to
save his life instead. But then stranger things had happened in these wild hills. Of that, Cole had no doubt.

O'Brian crawled to the campfire and helped himself to coffee. Neither man had much stomach for
food. O'Brian sat on a trunk-sized chunk of dolomite
and listened to the sound of rain mingle with the rushing falls.

"What do you make of him?" Cole asked, and in his youthful face, confusion reigned. He was uncertain of which course to take. He had expected to confront some sort of monster of the Ozarks and not the pitiful creature who looked hardly older than Cole, a victim of a terrible catastrophe that had left him mad perhaps, but no monster.

"I found these among his possibles," O'Brian said, and dumped the contents of a small leather bag on the floor of the cave. There was a pocket watch and three large opaque stones partly encrusted with kimberlite, a greenish-blue substance, claylike in consistency.

"Diamonds," O'Brian explained as he pointed to the stones. "Look at the back of the watch."

Cole turned the watch over in his hands and read the inscription.

> To Luther King
> on his 13th birthday
> 1860

"Luther." Cole raised his eyes to the man lying on the bedroll near the fire. The closed eyes fluttered for a moment, but the man remained asleep. "He could have found the watch," the Texan speculated, then shrugged. "But I guess it's as good a name as any for him." He fixed his gaze on the Osage Kid. "Question is, what'll we do now?"

"He's dying. Infection's already set in. Poison's at work. He needs better doctorin' than I can give,"

O'Brian said, running a hand through his black hair. "I reckon we could bring him to Little Rock. They got a hospital full of doctors. But you'll have to bring him in, 'cause I might run into Kedd." O'Brian drank his coffee and stared at the curtain of water outside.

O'Brian had been ready to avenge Katrina's death, had thought of nothing but revenge for the past four days of hard riding. But when the moment came, he had seen something of himself in Luther's ruined countenance. The Osage Kid knew what it was to be lost and friendless and hounded. There was no malice in such a wounded creature, only an animalistic fear and hurting.

Katrina's death had probably been a tragic accident. As for the other killings, O'Brian couldn't hazard a guess.

"Suppose the doctors in Little Rock get him well," Cole speculated. "It'll be for the hangman."

"More'n likely," O'Brian said. "Never heard of the law takin' kindly to folks who go around slittin' throats."

"I don't excuse him," Cole said. "And I'm not tryin' to act like no preacher, but maybe we ought to leave him be and let God do what needs to be done." Standing, he shoved his hands in his pockets and walked with long lazy strides to the mouth of the cave. The spray from the rushing water settled on his face and hands.

"Your father dead?"

"I don't know," O'Brian said. "He took off for the gold fields, promised he'd come back a rich man and take me and my mother away from the hills. I was six or thereabouts." The Osage finished his coffee, dumped the dregs out into the waterfall. "He was a big-hearted Irishman who meant well, but never returned."

"Well, I got a father. At least I reckon he's alive. Big John Anthem, that's what everybody calls him. I'm taller than him by half a foot." Cole chuckled and started back to the fire. "But he casts the bigger shadow," he warmly remembered. "And has a stubborn streak wide as the Mississippi."

"You got a family and a home waiting for you. Then what the hell are you doing here?" O'Brian exclaimed, anger in his voice.

Cole thought for a moment, knowing the answer deep in his heart. He had left home for the war determined to cover himself in glory, to return home a man of riches and distinction. But now he knew the glory of war is simply managing to survive, and wealth was relative. Sometimes being lucky enough to find a morsel of salt pork floating in his beans, or finding just the right pair of boots on a dead man were riches enough.

Cole had failed. But he was too proud to arrive home in defeat. A quarrel that had ended in a gunfight had accidentally brought Cole a bounty large enough to outfit himself. After that, Cole had decided that riding the trail of wanted men would be his ticket home. "What are you doing here?" O'Brian's question reverberated in his skull. Finally the Texan met the Osage's dark gaze.

"I'm waiting for Luther to die, same as you," Cole said.

The rain droned on. The hours crawled past. But neither man felt like sleeping. Luther's breathing was shallow, irregular, growing ever more labored. Still he clung to life with the stubbornness of a man pressing on because there is a task not yet completed . . .

21

Cole opened his eyes to study the sunlight streaming through the plunging falls that hid the entrance to the cave. It took him a moment to realize he had slept, and a moment more to fully comprehend he had dozed off in the presence of a killer. He bolted to his feet and swung around toward the blackened embers of the campfire. His gaze ranged over the rippled ceiling and smooth-worn walls of limestone bathed in a shimmering golden glow of diffused sunlight. The roan pawed at the cave floor and whinnied.

O'Brian's blankets were turned back, but looked rumpled and slept in. The Sharps had been set aside, its breech opened to reveal an empty chamber. The Osage Kid was not in the cave. Luther, sitting tensely upright, stared at the mouth of the cave. Sweat beaded the ragged latticework of scar tissue covering his forehead, his chest heaved in a succession of rapid breaths. His gaze never left the entrance, where the water tumbled through the overhang, but peered straight ahead as if he could see what lay outside the cave.

The hairs rose on the back of Cole's neck. Luther reminded the Texan of a trapped animal sensing danger. Cole picked up his carbine and, backing away from the wounded man, hurried to the entrance. He paused before edging out past the falls, to study the water-distorted images, then maneuvered himself just into the mist rising up from the spray where the waterfall crashed against the stony streambed.

O'Brian stood several yards downstream, in ankle-deep water, his right arm poised above his gun butt. Looking past him, Cole could barely distinguish a group of men on horseback spread out in a ragged line. Anthem hesitated, unable to decide whether or not he should show himself. Despite the noise of the falls, the cave acted as a sound chamber and Cole, with effort, heard and recognized the voice of Gage Bannister.

The creek bed rose sharply in a mass of broken rocks that increased in size and became two veritable battlements of lichen-covered limestone boulders that eventually gave way to forested hillsides. Bannister's voice reverberated among the steep walls and the bluff from which the waters of Buffalo Falls tumbled in a wavering cascade.

"Looking for something, Blue Elk?" Gage said.

"Dry kindling for a fire," O'Brian replied, cursing himself for his carelessness. His mind had been too preoccupied, he had forgotten to watch his back trail.

Well, nobody was perfect, he reflected. And nobody lived forever. "Surprised to see you, Gage. I'm a mite short on grub for breakfast. Hope you boys brought your own." His eyes settled on Kedd and his men. The presence of the Regulators worried O'Brian more than the likes of Ned Price, who walked his horse a few paces forward and trained his shotgun on him. "Appears you've taken on some new partners."

"A business arrangement," the gambler purred, his eyes bright behind the round wire-rim lenses. "Where's our killer?"

"Dead."

"And the Texan?"

"Dead," O'Brian remarked. He hoped Cole was awake and that Bannister's voice was carrying. He was going to need something other than a bluff to back him up.

"Too bad," Bannister said, mocking sympathy.

"Want me to finish the breed, Major?" Canton called out, whipping his Springfield up to his shoulder and sighting along the barrel. The corporal had no use for the Osage Kid.

"No," Bannister shouted.

"Not till he shows us the diamonds," Ned Price blurted out, then caught himself, too late, and suffered a blistering appraisal from Gage Bannister.

Canton looked over at Pepper Fisk, who shifted uneasily in the saddle, his breechloader in hand. "What diamonds?" the corporal asked, glancing from Bannister to Kedd, remembering that the two men had met privately.

"You were right, J. D." Fisk muttered.

Bannister groaned and glared at Price. "You stupid son of a bitch." He faced O'Brian again. There was no point in trying to conceal anything now. "Where are the diamonds?"

"Diamonds . . . ? Why, in the cave." O'Brian chuckled, thinking of the three meager stones he had discovered in Luther's pouch. As for the source of the stones, that was a location locked deep in the tortured recesses of the dying man's mind.

"Fair enough," Gage replied. He raised his Henry rifle.

"Hey, Major, I'm your prisoner, aren't I?" O'Brian called out, poised for action.

Andrew Kedd stroked his silver goatee a moment, then shook his head with a self-satisfied smile and answered, "I don't think I'm taking any prisoners today."

"Good-bye, breed," Bannister said.

Cole fired through the watery curtain. Unable to properly aim, he levered shot after shot in the direction of the horsemen. Horses reared and pawed the air in confusion. Price was thrown from the saddle and scampered for cover. The gully was filled with the thunderous exchange of gunfire. Bullets glanced off the rubble as O'Brian darted for the left bank. A slug ripped a bloody furrow across his thigh. Another ricocheted off his Navy Colt and knocked the weapon from his grasp. Bannister's men fired wildly, trying to hit the Osage while dodging the rain of bullets from the mouth of the cave. Cole rushed out of the mist and scrambled up into the battlements to the right as the wounded O'Brian reached the safety of the boulders to the left.

"Get them, you fools," Gage bellowed to the horsemen, who scattered to either side of the boulders. The gambler from Teardrop charged down the stream, peppering the rocks with his Henry as his horse plunged through the shallows. A fine watery mist exploded from his mount's driving hooves, drenching him to the bone.

Cole leapt up and chanced a shot. His Winchester spat flame and recoiled against his shoulder. Bannister twisted in the saddle as a slug from the Yellowboy shattered his side. The gambler tumbled out of the saddle and rolled over in the shallows, bruising his knees and peeling a layer of hide off his backside in the rocky creek bed. Cole chambered another shell and aimed, but he saw a shadow rise up from behind another boulder to his right. The Texan flung himself backward as Price's shotgun spewed buckshot and riddled the space he had just vacated.

Bannister staggered to his feet and limped toward the cave, only one thing on his mind: let the others kill themselves. He couldn't be bothered now.

Cole rolled in between two massive stones and began to climb, trying to work himself higher than Shotgun Price. He squirmed underneath a boulder that had tumbled down from the bluff above and come to rest against a second stone forming a natural bridge.

"There's more where that came from," Price's voice drifted across the creek bank. Cole continued to crawl, cautiously working his way upstream. He wondered if O'Brian had been hit bad. Cole reckoned he'd find out soon enough. He found a man-sized crevice in the weathered stone and paused in it to reload, sliding shell after shell into the carbine.

At close range Price's shotgun had a distinct advantage. So the sensible thing was to keep his distance from him. That was the cautious thing to do. But then caution might prolong things and Cole Anthem came from impatient stock.

"You're a dead man," Price's voice carried to him.

Not dead yet, Cole silently answered.

Canton followed the major as the officer scrambled out of the rocks and entered the woods. Sunlight slanted through the branches of hickory and oak, and brown wrens fluttered through its rays. A copperhead slithered out of harm's way and lost itself among yellow-green ferns crowding a nearby clearing. Overhead a woodpecker attacked its oak with all the fury of some miniature lumberman, hacking away at the bark in its quest for grubs and wood ants.

Canton, still gasping from a climb up the bank, caught up with Kedd, placed a big beefy hand on the major's shoulder, and spun him around.

Kedd's cheeks reddened with anger. He was as winded from the flight as the corporal, but the officer refused to show it. Kedd drew himself upright. "How dare you, Corporal," the major snapped. He was already furious. His hat with the black plume had been trampled in the creek bed.

"What diamonds? You and that goddamn gambler was fixin' to pull one over on me and Pepper, eh, major?" The corporal balanced his rifle in his right hand. His sideburns seemed to bristle like the hackles of a wolf.

"You lay a hand on me again, Corporal, and I will shoot you dead," Andrew Kedd calmly warned, revolver in hand. He knew he no longer cut a fine figure. Last night's downpour had reduced him to a muddy and miserable state, but he was still the officer in command and would be treated as such. "You'll follow orders and do as you're told," Kedd added.

"You ain't no officer now, Mr. Kedd, you ain't no gentleman either, no, sirree." Canton laughed. "You're just another greedy bastard like myself." Canton's foul breath fanned Kedd's face. "Now tell me what the devil is going on."

"You're mad," Kedd said, and started down a deer trail that wound its way among the trees. Canton's hand shot out, grabbed Kedd by the shoulder, and spun him around once again.

"Don't you walk away from me," the corporal growled.

Andrew Kedd's Colt Dragoon bucked in his slim fist, and Canton staggered back against an oak, glanced off the trunk, and dropped his rifle.

"My God, you've shot me," the corporal groaned. As he staggered toward the embankment, the incline speeded his stumbling pace. Blood seeped from the hole in his back where the slug had exited, tearing out a fist-sized chunk of flesh in the process. Kedd stared in disbelief at the smoking revolver in his hand. Canton buckled and pitched forward, his body airborne for a few brief seconds before it crashed onto the rocks below, spooking the Regulators' already skittish horses.

"They'll frown on that in Little Rock," O'Brian said, emerging from a grove of dogwoods. His trouser leg was blood-soaked, but he'd fixed a tourniquet above the flesh wound. "Drop the gun, Major."

Kedd laughed softly, his back to the Osage Kid. "I saw you lose your gun in the creek below," he said slowly. "I'm calling your bluff." The major whirled to face O'Brian, but stiffened as he saw there was another gun gripped in the Osage's right hand. The shortened barrel was aimed, unsteadily, at Kedd's chest.

The major's face flushed with anger and his eyes bulged as he loosed a furious cry and charged, his gun spewing flame and black smoke. O'Brian had dropped to the ground and with a two-handed grip trained the shortened barrel of his Navy Colt on Kedd, a dozen yards away. He fired two evenly spaced shots, his gun jumping in his firm grip.

The major slid to a halt as if he had run into a wall. His entire body trembled, his back arched. O'Brian fired again. Kedd clutched at his chest, fell against the trunk of an oak tree, and slid to a sitting position at the base of the trunk. He stared at O'Brian, who clambered to his feet and advanced on the officer. Slowly, Kedd's hand fell away and his eyes dulled, the jaws went slack and his head hung to one side.

O'Brian spun as a twig popped behind him. Standing between the hickories, Pepper Fisk froze and dropped his rifle as a frightened expression transformed his homely features. O'Brian lowered the Colt and waited for the Regulator to make his play.

"I could sure use a drink," Fisk said in a dry rasping tone. He smacked his lips and tried to look harmless.

"I hear there's plenty of saloons in Colorado. Maybe you ought to go see for yourself," O'Brian said.

Fisk nodded and retreated into the forest. He had his life and a horse. What more could a man ask for? The private decided he couldn't be out of these hills too soon.

Shotgun Ned Price was a born tracker. It was said he could read sign over barren ground. Price paused and chose his steps wisely, taking care not to alert the young Texan hidden in the cul-de-sac on the other side of the limestone ledge. Ten minutes earlier, Price had caught a glimpse of sunlight reflected off Cole's Winchester's brass frame.

That single glimpse had told the gunman all he needed to know. The Texan must have worked his way downstream and taken a position behind Price, planning no doubt to pick Ned off when he returned for his horse. But Price had slipped around behind young Anthem and turned the tables on the Texan.

A lizard scurried across the boulder and Price drew his hand away, mistaking the creature for a snake. He

watched a scorpion scuttle out from under a loose pile
of rocks and he crushed the insect beneath his boot.
Cautiously, he listened, but heard only the cascading
water. Tucking the shotgun against his chest, he eased
the hammers back to cock the weapon. He waited
then, wanting the Texan to sweat a little. Price stared
up at the fiercely blue sky, so pure and clear with only
an occasional smudge of slate-gray cloud, the last ves-
tiges of the previous day's storm.

Price counted off another minute and decided it
was time. He edged around the boulder, paused at the
narrow entrance to the cul-de-sac, then darted out and
loosed one barrel of buckshot down the corridor between two walls of limestone. The shotgun sounded
like a cannon in the narrow confines. The Winchester
'66 clattered to the ground in a cloud of splintered
stone. Save for the carbine, the cul-de-sac was empty.

"Shit!" Price said, a sickening feeling in his gut. A
shadow fell across the stone behind him: Anthem
trained his Navy Colt on the gunman.

"Don't make me kill you," Cole said. "Walk away
from this. Just leave your guns and walk out of here."

Price whirled and fired, blasting a chunk out of a
limestone boulder. Cole loosed a shot in return and
dusted the gunman's coat. The bullet flattened against
Ned's sternum and ripped up through his throat. The
gunman flew backward into the cul-de-sac, dead as he
hit the ground.

Cole holstered the Colt and, stepping over the
body, retrieved his Winchester. His youthful features

betrayed his distaste and a sense of outrage at the waste of it all.

Bannister's eyes slowly adjusted to the cave. His spectacles were twisted; only one lens remained and it was cracked. He stumbled and bit his lip to keep from crying out as the pain of his wounded side and twisted ankle overwhelmed him.

Gage felt along the walls, trying to find a telltale seam of kimberlite that would yield the expected fortune. But the walls were smooth-worn, slippery to the touch. Maybe the floor then.

He knelt and began crawling. Again, smooth dolomite, nothing but water-eroded stone. Maybe this cave wasn't the source of the gems. No, it had to be. It had to be. He crawled over the bedrolls, kicked the blankets aside. He accidentally put his hand in the blackened circle of the campfire and drew away, grimacing in agony from the bite of still-warm embers. The palm of his hand was blistered.

"Where are they?" he yelled, and his voice echoed in the chamber. He squinted, and in his near-blind state espied the leather pouch lying in the center of a blanket near the remnants of the campfire.

Bannister grabbed the bag, ripped it open, and dumped the contents out onto the blanket. He ignored the watch and reached for the three raw gems. Just three . . . But where did they come from? Where the blasted hell did they come from?

Luther seemed to materialize out of the blackness at the rear of the cave. He was dying and every step took a maximum of effort, but Bannister was too pre-occupied to notice him. Luther had seen his face. He recognized the man, remembered with a young boy's mind and a boy's fear. Here was the fourth man, the last of the four who had killed his father.

Luther paused, rocking on his heels as he fought to maintain his balance. He held a broad-bladed, jagged-edged knife. His arm raised. Move forward now, just another step. The snake in his belly would not let him die. One step more. He is the last. And after it is done you can rest. So tired. Tired. After it is done you can be with your father.

Gage Bannister realized for the first time he wasn't alone. He squinted, tried to focus on the figure standing over him. Kedd? Price?

"Who are you?" the gambler from Teardrop asked in a halting voice.

With a glitter of steel, the knife swept down. One moment for shock, a flash of indecision, then Bannister rolled over on his back as Luther's great weight fell atop him, the knife shattered at the hilt as the blade glanced off the floor. Once powerful hands clawed for the gambler's throat. Gage shrieked and fought free of the dying man's grasp. He scrambled across the floor of the cave, tearing his trousers, smearing his coat. With the wall at his back, Bannister dragged his revolver from its holster and aimed it at the massive shape. Yet he held his fire as Luther slowly pushed himself off the floor, then collapsed once again, his arm outstretched in death, still trying to avenge himself on the last of his father's murderers.

Bannister laughed softly and scrambled to his feet. He wiped his face on his forearm. The fear in him was slowly ebbing.

"Not today. Not ever, you son of a bitch." He staggered toward the curtain of water, anxious to be out of the cave and away from its monstrous inhabitant.

He cleared the falls, emerged from the spray into sunlight. He was battered and disgusted and in no mood to be confronted by Anthem.

The young Texan waited, his Winchester Yellowboy gripped loosely in his right hand. He stood in the shallows of the creek, his long reflection stretching out across the water. On the other side of Anthem, the gambler's horse cropped at the grasses sprouting among the boulders.

"Get out of my way," Bannister said.

Cole did not reply. Nor did he move. And his youthful features darkened, his cold-eyed stare showing as much warmth as a winter norther.

The gambler removed his shattered eyeglasses and rubbed the crease on his nose.

"I can see well enough to drop you, boy," Bannister said. He had another pair of spectacles in his saddlebag. "Stand aside, dammit." The gambler was anxious to get the hell out. It was only a few yards to his horse. He laughed brusquely. "Are you really any good with that carbine?" he asked Cole. Then he made his move.

Cole shouldered his rifle, fired, levered a shell, and the Yellowboy roared again, reverberating throughout the creek bed. Bannister rocked on his heels, slugs tearing into his broad chest, hammering him back into the cascading falls. The plunging water drove the gambler to his knees. Cole fired again and Bannister collapsed facedown in the creek.

The young Texan looked down at the carbine in his hands, then at Bannister.

"I can make it dance," said Anthem.

22

As Cole Tyler Anthem and Blue Elk O'Brian rode out of the valley, a freshening breeze washed the air of gunsmoke and leeched the gloom from their hearts and minds. Five graves lay behind them, scratched out of the hard earth of the Ozarks.

Spring had finally come to this broken land. The season of timeless affirmation, which promised that, for all the dark deeds of men, the world could be a warm and wondrous place and life, for all its harshness, could be renewed.

O'Brian reined to a halt on the crest of a hump-backed ridge that angled off toward the mouth of yet another valley.

"You sure you don't need a doctor," Cole asked as he pulled alongside the Osage.

"Nah," O'Brian said, checking the wound. "I just lost some hide. It isn't the first time." He studied the trail leading east and back to Teardrop. Then he looked to the west, an idea tempting him.

"Reckon I'll leave these hills to the ghosts," O'Brian added. The spirit of his mother's people would always be here, and the land would always belong to the Osage no matter who lived on it, no matter how many towns were built in the years to come. O'Brian grinned. "Pass my regards along to Mindy Lou Harlowe. I'll bet her welcomes are even sweeter than her good-byes." His gray eyes twinkled and he laughed heartily at Cole's embarrassment. "That gal has a snare set just for you, Anthem." At a touch of his heels the chestnut gelding started down the slope. O'Brian let the sun lead the way. "Of course you could ride along with me for a spell."

"Ride where?" Cole shouted.

O'Brian waved a hand in a gesture that encompassed the entire western horizon with its forested hills and the bluffs beyond, sunswept meadows and endless plains.

"Out there," he said.

Anthem looked over his shoulder, east toward Teardrop, then west again to where the clouds cast shadows upon the land.

Ahead, the Osage Kid paused, skylined on a ridge.

And Cole Tyler Anthem rode toward him, drawn to the ridge and the emerald hills, and farther, to the frontier, wild and free, where adventure awaited and trails had no end.

**HE LEFT HOME A BOY.
RETURNED A MAN.
AND RODE OUT AGAIN A RENEGADE ...**

TEXAS ANTHEM

KERRY NEWCOMB

AT THE BONNET RANCH, they thought Johnny Anthem had died on the Mexican border. But then Anthem came home, escaped from the living hell of a Mexican prison, and returned to find the woman he loved married to the man who betrayed him. For Johnny Anthem, the time had come to face his betrayer, to stand up to the powerful rancher who had raised him as his own son, and to fight for the only love of his life.

"Kerry Newcomb is one of those writers who lets you know from his very first lines that you're in for a ride. And he keeps his promise . . . Newcomb knows what he is doing, and does it enviably well."
—Cameron Judd, author of *Confederate Gold*

**AVAILABLE WHEREVER BOOKS ARE SOLD FROM
ST. MARTIN'S PAPERBACKS**

SOME CALLED HIM THEIR CAPTAIN.
SOME CALLED HIM THEIR ENEMY.
SOME CALLED HIM THE DEVIL HIMSELF . . .

MAD MORGAN

KERRY NEWCOMB

He came out of Cuba's bloody sugar cane fields, a young Welshman who had been kidnapped from his home and forced into barbaric slavery in the New World. Then on a black night, Henry Morgan made his escape, and soon was commanding a former prison bark manned by criminals, misfits and adventurers—men who owed Mad Morgan their freedom, their loyalty, and their lives.

"Awash with treachery and romance, this well-spun yarn fairly crackles with danger and suspense . . . Colorful, old-fashioned adventure [and] vigorous historical fiction."
—*Booklist*

AVAILABLE WHEREVER BOOKS ARE SOLD FROM
ST. MARTIN'S PAPERBACKS